Secrets...hopes...dreams...

Welcome to

*Silver *Spires

where

School Friends
are
forever!

Collect the *School Friends* series:

Welcome to Silver Spires
Drama at Silver Spires
 Rivalry at Silver Spires
Princess at Silver Spires
Secrets at Silver Spires
Star of Silver Spires

Drama at Silver Spires

Ann Bryant

USBORNE

For my faithful and discerning first reader
and wonderful daughter, Jody

My grateful thanks to Ginny Whitelaw
for all her invaluable help

First published in the UK in 2008 by Usborne Publishing Ltd.,
Usborne House, 83-85 Saffron Hill, London EC1N 8RT, England.
www.usborne.com

Series cover design by Sally Griffin
Cover illustration by Suzanne Sales/New Division

The name Usborne and the devices ♀ 🎈 are Trade Marks of
Usborne Publishing Ltd.

A CIP catalogue record for this book is available from the British Library.

First published in America in 2012 AE.
PB ISBN 9780794531478   ALB ISBN 9781601302700
JF AMJJASOND/12   01564/2
Printed in Dongguan, Guangdong, China.

Chapter One

I was staring into the distance with a massive smile on my face, imagining myself on a stage somewhere on Broadway. The sound of applause was ringing around the auditorium, and I felt the waves of adoration rolling over me as I took yet another bow. But then this totally cool daydream was interrupted by the sound of my best friend, Mia, whispering my name urgently and tapping me on the leg.

"Georgie!"

I came back to earth with an ugly thud, realizing I wasn't on a stage at all. I was in my school assembly and the principal, Ms. Carmichael, was saying the prayer while every single one of the 360 girls in the hall was bowing her head respectfully. Well, every one except me. I quickly looked down and tried to get myself back into the daydream but got distracted by the sight of a run in my tights. It definitely hadn't been there first thing this morning. I know that for a fact, because Miss Jennings would have spotted it with her eagle eye and made me go back to the dorm to change into a new pair of tights immediately.

Good old Miss Jennings. She's the dorm supervisor at Hazeldean, which is my boarding house at Silver Spires school. Most people find her really strict, and it's true that she keeps her face straight the whole time, which Mia says is totally scary, but personally I like her. The secret is to chit-chat with her lots and tell her jokes and then you can get a smile out of her. Well, *I* can anyway.

Yes I *can*! That makes two things I'm talented at. Acting and getting a smile out of Miss Jennings. Hallelujah! I tell you, it's tough being in a dorm with five other girls who are all completely gorgeous and talented. I mean, take Mia. She came to Silver Spires on a music scholarship because she's so wonderful at piano. Then there's Grace – she got a sports scholarship. As for Jess, she'd definitely have an art scholarship if there *was* such a thing. And

Katy…well she's the trendiest babe on this planet – I'd love to look like Katy – and we all just know she'll finish up as a fashion designer because her sketches are amazing and she's obsessed with the whole fashion scene. And finally – and this is the big one – there's Naomi, who is an African princess. She's also extremely beautiful and very wise. It's just not fair that *all* of them are talented. I mean, how am I supposed to compete with that bunch? They're all my friends and I love them to death, but I sometimes wish they weren't quite so impressive.

Seriously, the only thing I'm good at is acting. Drama has always been my passion. Even when I was only two and a half I used to love dressing up and stuff. My mom said I would stand in the middle of the circle of mothers at play group, wearing an apron from the dress-up box, and entertain everyone by pretending to scrub the floor. Thinking about it, I wonder if I might have developed a bit of a Cinderella obsession, but I don't see how I could have understood the story if I was only two and a half. Aha! Maybe I really am a very smart person but nobody has managed to bring it out of me yet.

"Amen."

Whoops! I think I must have been in another daydream. Anyway, now Ms. Carmichael had finished the prayer we only had the teachers' announcements to go, or notices, as everyone calls them. I wonder why they're called notices when they're not written down. And I also wonder if anyone ever listens to them. I looked around and wasn't surprised to see that most people seemed to have glazed over. Assemblies are probably the most boring part of boarding-school life. Oh and science, and geography...and history. Actually, I can't say I'm a big fan of any classes except drama. The drama class and drama club are the biggest highlights of my week, well, apart from watching *The Fast Lane* on TV, which is my fave program ever. Drama even beats eating smuggled cookies after lights out and stifling giggles with my friends in case Miss Carol, the dorm mom, hears, or going shopping at the beginning of school before you've spent all your allowance. Now, come to think about it, there are hundreds of highlights to boarding-school life – well, to Silver Spires life anyway. Silver Spires is the best school in the world, in case I didn't mention that.

"Georgie!"

Mia was bashing my leg again, but this time when she said my name it didn't sound like a telling-off. In fact for some reason or other Mia was pretty excited. I tuned into what was happening and realized that Miss Pritchard, the senior drama teacher, was standing up. It's funny because the hall was already silent but it went into an even deeper silence when Miss Pritchard began to speak. And personally I went into ecstasy.

"Some of you will know that the junior play will be staged before Christmas break. Anyone in sixth, seventh or eighth grade can audition. The play is called *Castles in the Air* and it's based on the book *Little Women* by Louisa M. Alcott."

My heart hammered with excitement. A play. How fantastic is that? And *Little Women* is my favorite book ever.

"I'm sure many of you have read the book," went on Miss Pritchard, "and know that the story is centered around four sisters: Meg, Jo, Beth and Amy."

Just hearing those four names felt magical, especially the name Amy. That was the sister I always liked reading about the most.

"There are quite a few other substantial roles in the play as well as these four main ones, and there are also lots of smaller roles." Miss Pritchard paused and smiled around at everyone, and I smiled right back. I was suddenly Cinderella again and she was my fairy godmother – *You shall go to the ball!*

I hung on to her every word because I didn't want to miss a thing or get anything wrong. It would be terrible if I didn't show up at the auditions because I hadn't heard the time right.

"There's a very high standard of acting at Silver Spires, and traditionally this junior play has always been incredibly well received by the parents, which is important because it's a showcase for the school..." She smiled again but then suddenly looked very serious and spoke in a slow, firm voice. "To produce a fine performance I need total commitment from my actors..."

I stood up straight and stuck out my chin. She could rely on *me*, all right. I'd learn all my words overnight and turn up at every rehearsal right on time. I couldn't wait to get started, in fact. *Come on, Miss Pritchard, tell us when the auditions are...*

"So bear that in mind if you're thinking of auditioning for a part. It's great fun being involved in a theater production but it's also hard work and there are sacrifices to be made, such as missing your favorite clubs sometimes, missing television to learn your lines..."

I didn't care. I'd miss every meal as well, if she wanted me to, even though the meals at Silver Spires are mouth-wateringly yum-worthy and eating is one of my favorite activities in the whole world.

"If you'd like to audition for a part you'll need to come to the senior hall, which, for sixth grade students who don't do drama club, is upstairs and along the main corridor in this building..."

She pointed to the ceiling, and I thought back to my first day at Silver Spires when I'd gone exploring for anything to do with drama, and first come across the senior hall and also seen the incredible new theater, which looked like something out of Broadway in New York. It would be so fantastic to perform on that stage.

"I'm going to be doing auditions for eighth graders during their drama classes on Thursday, and for sixth and seventh graders after school on Thursday, which gives you a few days to prepare yourselves. I've run off copies of mini-scripts and they're on my desk in my office, which is next to the hall. You can help yourselves to those. Choose a speech by the character you want to audition for, but also come armed with an idea of another role you might be interested in, because, of course, you're not necessarily going to be lucky enough to get the first part you want."

Miss Pritchard sat down and Ms. Carmichael

nodded at the music teacher, who pressed play on the CD, and the next minute the hall was filled with some beautiful violin music, or was it cello? Who cared? I just wanted to push past everyone filing out neatly row by row, get a hold of a script and take it to the dorm, then spend the whole day flopped on my bed learning every single word of every single part.

"Bet *you're* happy!" said Mia, tucking her arm through mine when we finally got out of the hall.

"You are *so* right! I am in fact the happiest girl on the planet!" I gabbled as I pulled away and rushed upstairs, taking two steps at a time.

Grabbing a script from the desk in Miss Pritchard's office, I started reading it immediately so I had to walk very slowly to make sure I didn't fall or walk into anyone as I went back downstairs to my friends.

Mia put her arm around me as we left the main building and Grace patted me on the back. "Smooth moves, Georgie! I've never seen you go upstairs so fast!"

Katy laughed. "And look! She's actually concentrating on something. This must be serious!"

"Yes, and it's not easy concentrating with everyone talking!" I said, throwing her an annoyed look, which I quickly turned into a grin because how could I feel annoyed when every single nerve and tendon and sinew and all those other scientific parts of the human body that have always been a mystery to me were glowing brightly and lighting up my life? "I'm going for the part of Amy!" I announced in a voice that came out squeaky with excitement.

It felt so great to hear those words hanging in the air after I'd spoken them that I repeated the main one three times. "Amy, Amy, Amy!" Which made everyone giggle. But then Naomi gently reminded us that hanging around waiting for me to collect the script had made us late for science and we ought to get a move on. So we put on a little spurt and caught up with a group of seventh grade girls just ahead. I was still at the back though, walking slowly so I could read the script at the same time.

"I've never read *Little Women*," I heard Jess say. Then she called back to me, "What's it about? Who's Amy?"

My mind went straight back to the time when I was nine and I got the book in my Christmas stocking. I hadn't wanted to read it at first because it looked so old-fashioned, but Mom had actually sat me down and read the first chapter out loud, and after that I'd been hooked. I remember how I used to keep turning to the front cover to take another look at the picture of the sisters, and even now I can visualize Amy, clear as anything. She had blonde hair that curled at the bottom, blue eyes and a mischievous kind of smile, a little like my younger sister, Roxanne. My hair is a sort of medium brown color and it's just long enough to put in a ponytail without having any short pieces hanging out. It's pretty thick. I used to wish it wasn't, but actually, now I think about it, Amy's hair looks pretty thick. If only I was blonde, that would be even better.

I sighed a happy sigh and caught up with the others. "She's the youngest of the four March sisters and she's bright and bubbly…"

"Like *you*, Georgie!" laughed Naomi. "Typecasting! Terrific!"

"And she's also very artistic, which I know *isn't* like me," I quickly pointed out. "But that's what acting's all about." Then I suddenly realized there was something I hadn't found out. "Are any of you guys going to audition?"

They all started gabbling away at once so I couldn't make out what any of them was saying, but I got the general idea that nobody was that big on the thought of acting.

"I wonder if the students can help paint the sets and scenery for the stage," said Jess, looking thoughtful.

Katy fell into step beside her. "I think I'll find out

who's in charge of costumes. I'd love to be—"

One of the seventh grade girls we were passing flung a very haughty look in our direction and interrupted Katy in a know-it-all voice. "Mrs. Chambers is in charge of the wardrobe department, actually, but she won't let you help. She only lets eighth graders."

Katy looked disappointed and Naomi obviously felt sorry for her. "You can always ask, anyway, Kates," she said quietly. "But we'd better go now or we'll be late…"

"See you back at Hazeldean, you two," Mia called over her shoulder as she and Grace went jogging off to their lab with Naomi and Katy, because the four of them all have science together.

Jess and I kept walking with the seventh graders and I wished I had the guts to turn to the know-it-all girl and say, "Did you write the book of life or something?" But sixth graders don't talk to seventh graders like that. You just don't.

"Do the students get to help with the set?" Jess asked her.

The girl shrugged and the expression on her face said she couldn't care less about such a trivial little thing. "You'll have to check with the art department. I'm an actor."

Jess said, "Right," then stopped walking as she seemed to suddenly remember something. "Oh no!" she said. "I've totally forgotten my science textbook – I'll have to run back and get it. Save me a place, Georgie, okay?" And off she went.

As soon as she'd gone, *Miss Know-It-All* nodded at the script I was clutching. "So what part are you going for?"

"Amy."

"Amy!" She did a little snort of laughter as though I'd announced that I intended to be the director or something.

Then all her friends started smirking. One of them turned to the know-it-all girl and said, "Wooo, competition for you, Cara," in a sarcastic tone of voice, which made everyone burst into laughter. And another girl rolled her eyes and said, "As if!" which really made my hackles rise.

"What's so funny?" I asked.

"Sorry," said Cara, shaking her head slowly. "I shouldn't laugh really because you wouldn't know, being a sixth grader…"

I didn't like the way she flashed her eyes around all the time she was talking, like she was checking that everyone was still looking at her.

"Know *what*?"

"Well…" She sighed, and spoke really slowly as though all sixth graders were preschoolers. "I mean…you did realize that Amy is one of the four main roles, didn't you? Sorry, what's your name?"

"Georgie." Then I was suddenly sick of being patronized. "Course I realized. I'm not stupid. Anyway, are *you* going to audition?"

She exchanged a look with one of her friends and it was the friend who answered. "Obviously. She's the best actress in Silver Spires. She had a main part in last year's play even though she was only a sixth grader, you know. And that *never* happens."

"So, what part are you going for?" I asked casually.

She reached into her pocket and I wondered for a second whether she'd written it down for some unknown reason, but then she pulled out a little tin, undid it and smeared lipgloss onto her lips. At that moment she just seemed to love herself so much that I really hated her, even though I hardly knew her. It wasn't till she'd put the tin back and rubbed her lips together that she finally deigned to look at me. "Amy," came the answer. She smiled mockingly and my heart sank, but then I tried to give myself a pep talk. Just because everyone thought Cara was a really good actress, it didn't mean that she'd automatically get the part of Amy, did it? And anyway, who was to say she was any better than me? I'd had big parts in every single play at elementary school, starting from when I was the enormous turnip in the harvest festival in kindergarten, to when I played Nick Bottom in *A Midsummer Night's Dream* in fifth grade.

We'd arrived at the science classroom so I gave Cara the coolest look I could manage while I tried to think of some clever parting line, but then I realized her eyes were on my right leg and she was trying to stop herself from smirking. I guessed she was looking at the run in my tights and I made the mistake of glancing down and saw that the stupid thing had risen from my ankle to just above my knee, getting wider and wider as it went up. Normally I don't care about things like that but I did at this moment. It made me feel stupid.

"It's only a run, you know!" said my big mouth before my brain had chance to stop it.

She just stared at me as though I was pathetic.

"See you at the auditions then," I said casually.

She still didn't answer, and as I went into the science classroom my ears were on full alert, listening out for snickers. I didn't hear any, but that's not to say the oh-so-clever Cara wasn't smirking and exchanging looks with her friends. I tell you, it was a big relief when the door closed behind me.

Chapter Two

"She makes me sick!"

"Just ignore her, Georgie. The only thing you need to worry about is doing your best at the audition."

That was Naomi. She always comes out with wise things like that. I gave her the best smile I could manage, because it's not easy smiling when you're feeling irritable, and I'd gotten myself really worked up about stupid Cara.

"The thing is, I really *really* want the part of Amy," I said with a big sigh. "I'm just like Amy. The part was totally made for me!" But even as I was saying it, I didn't think any of my friends could possibly realize just how much I meant it. "I want it more than anything in the world," I added, to help them get the picture.

"Well you've got just as much chance as Cara," said Mia, putting her arm around me.

The six of us were sitting on the circular rug in the middle of the dorm in our jammies. I'd been thinking about cocky Cara all day long but this was the first chance I'd had to have a real conversation about her, because my friends are always rushing off somewhere like volleyball practice or debate club or the computer room or piano practice or art club. They're just so busy, even though I've told them they're crazy and they ought to be more like me and go to chill club, which actually means don't go to any club at all but just chill out. No, seriously, the only *real* club I do is drama. Unfortunately, though, it's not as good as I thought it would be because we're always having to get in groups and do improvisations, making something up as we go along, rather than following a script. There's nothing wrong with that, I know, but the trouble is I'm always bursting with ideas about what my group could do, and it's so frustrating when I have to shut up because we're supposed to take turns to be the director. I can't wait till eighth grade. Miss Pritchard does drama in eighth, ninth and tenth grade, and everyone says the classes and clubs are amazing.

"I wish you'd heard the way Cara was talking," I said, in a rather sulky voice. "She thinks she's so smart and all her friends think she's queen bee. I mean, she looked at me like I was completely dumb. And imagine asking me if I realized that Amy was a main part!" I put on a snooty showy-offy voice to imitate her. "Woo-hoo, look at *me*! I'm an *actor*!"

Mia immediately broke into giggles, which set the others off.

It was Grace who recovered first. "What made you so crazy about acting in the first place, Georgie? Or did you just kind of realize you were good at it?"

I love talking about my favorite subject, so my irritation with Cara soon melted away. "Well... I've always loved acting, but when I was eight..." I felt on top of the world as my mind filled up with the coolest memory of a golden theater. "Mom and Dad took me to see the play of *The Witches* – you know the Roald Dahl story – in New York. I remember Roxanne falling asleep, but then she was only little. I'd seen pantomimes before that, and one musical, but I'd never seen an actual play, and something just kind of clicked inside me because it all made perfect sense, even though the characters and the setting were nothing like I'd imagined them in the book."

I stopped talking and saw that my friends were looking totally gobsmacked.

"Georgie!" said Mia. "I knew you loved drama and everything, but I never realized until now just how serious you are about it all!"

"Me neither!" said Katy. "I think that's the first time I've ever heard you actually being totally serious!"

"I think it's really interesting," said Naomi, frowning. "What do you think about movies?"

I was so loving this conversation with my friends taking me seriously for a change. I know they usually think I'm totally laid-back. That's because I'm not that good at schoolwork so I pretend I don't care too much about it, otherwise it would be embarrassing to try so hard and get such lame results. Plus, I'm also terrible at sports and anything energetic. But acting is my big passion and always will be.

At that moment I noticed Grace sneak a little look at her watch, and it was obviously catching because next thing they were all at it.

"Better go to the bathroom," said Grace. "It's nearly nine. Miss Jennings will be here in a sec." And everyone started to get up.

But I didn't want the conversation to end yet so I spoke at about a hundred miles an hour before they all disappeared. "Movies-are-completely-different-from-the-theater-*and*-from-books, Naomi." There was a knock at the door and I knew it would be Miss Jennings.

"We'll talk in bed," whispered Naomi.

But I was desperate to finish what I was saying so I talked even faster until the words all tumbled into each other. "'Coseverythinghappensintheblinkofan eyeinmovies...'"

And we all burst out laughing, even me, which was how Miss Jennings found us when she opened the door.

"What's the cause of all the hilarity?" she asked, looking around suspiciously as the others grabbed their toothbrushes and toothpaste and rushed off to the bathroom. Then she gave me what I call her dry look. "Why are you sitting in the middle of the room instead of getting ready for bed, young lady?"

Mia hung back. "Georgie's excited about auditioning for a main part in the junior play, Miss Jennings."

"I see. Well, I can tell you that Miss Pritchard doesn't put up with any nonsense, you know. Come on, Georgie! Chop-chop!"

"I won't give her any nonsense," I said, flashing my biggest smile at Miss Jennings.

She didn't smile back, just looked around our dorm and spoke extra briskly. "Bathroom. Now!" But her eyes definitely twinkled as I scuttled past her with my washbag.

Later, when I was lying in bed, I realized Miss Jennings hadn't actually made any comment about me auditioning for a big role, apart from what she said about Miss Pritchard. And I felt a stab of anxiety in case she thought it wasn't worth saying anything as I'm only in sixth grade, and not likely to get a main part.

I knew really that it was only one of those silly nighttime thoughts, because Miss Jennings would hardly start chatting when it was time for bed, and anyway, it was a good thing that she'd not made a comment because that showed she thought it was perfectly natural for me to audition for a main part. After all, Cara got a main part when she was only a sixth grader, didn't she? So why shouldn't I? Yes, I would just shock everyone by being absolutely stunningly fantastic at the auditions.

There was a niggling thought at the back of my tired mind trying to point out that I had to be better than Cara if I wanted to get the part of Amy, and that maybe I ought to think of another part. But I had set my heart on Amy and nothing else would do, so I ignored the thought and instead went into a beautiful daydream about Mom and Dad and Roxanne sitting proudly in the audience with Grandma, and everyone clapping their heads off, or maybe that should be clapping their hands off...

I was practically asleep but something made me snap on my little night-light and pull my script out from under my pillow.

"Don't suppose anyone wants to test me on my speech?" I whispered into the gloom, but they must have all been in the land of snooze, so I tested myself and finished up by reading through the whole script again. It was nearly eleven o'clock when I finally switched off the light.

The next morning I felt so full of happiness about the auditions being one day closer that I shot out of bed and off to the bathroom in about two seconds flat, which earned me a round of applause from the others as I'm usually the last up. When we were getting ready to leave for breakfast I suddenly had the urge to get a hold of a copy of *Little Women* so I could have that great feeling I always get when I read the book and find myself in the world of the four sisters, imagining myself as Amy. I also wanted to recall every single bit of the story, because the mini-scripts that Miss Pritchard gave us were a short version of the whole play, just for learning parts for the auditions.

There's a small library in one of the common rooms, which consists of a few shelves of books that no one ever looks at. At least *I* don't. But right then I felt like the biggest bookworm in the world, because I was so dying to read *Little Women.* It was the one and only book I'd ever actually noticed in the common room, because I remember thinking that the front cover was really plain compared to the cover of the version that I had at home.

In the common room I scanned the books on all three shelves as fast as I could, expecting to see *Little Women* immediately, but it wasn't there, which made me panic slightly because I'd set my heart on reading it before Thursday. So then I decided to slow down and look carefully because I must have missed it. No one ever takes these books out. *Do* they? I crossed my fingers as I examined every title on the top shelf.

Please let it be here somewhere. Please let it... But it wasn't, so I started on the second shelf, still praying hard, and it wasn't there either. By the time I'd done the last shelf my spirits had sunk down to Australia.

I walked over to breakfast in a bad mood, but by the time I joined the line for hot meals, I'd had an inspirational idea. I could go to the library in the English wing right after breakfast. There would most likely be a copy in there. I'd be a little late for double math, which was the first class, but I could probably get Jess to give some excuse to Mr. Ledbetter for me. I knew she wouldn't be over the moon about that idea though, because it wasn't the first time I'd asked her, as I don't like being on time for math or it lasts so long I always think I'm going to die of boredom.

When I had my bacon, egg and mushrooms, I looked around the massive cafeteria for my friends and spotted Mia's back with her long blonde ponytail hanging neatly down the middle. At that very moment she turned around and smiled, and that took me right back to something that happened before I even joined Silver Spires. It was on orientation day, before summer, but I can remember it like yesterday. We were all gathered in the hall with our parents, just kind of milling around waiting until everyone had turned up, and I decided to play a game that I sometimes play when I wish I could see into the future. I said to myself, *Okay, if that girl with the long blonde hair turns around before I've counted to seven* (my lucky number), *it means it's going to be good at this school.*

And like some kind of miracle, she not only turned around on six, but looked right at me and gave me a shaky smile. I was so made up with this result that I grinned at her like a Cheshire cat, and that was the beginning of our friendship.

I told Mia my library plan as I gobbled down my delicious breakfast and Grace tried to make me slow down.

"You can't be digesting it that way," she said with a worried frown.

"And the faster you eat the sooner you'll find yourself hungry again," Naomi warned me, with a slightly disapproving look.

I didn't reply because I'd been looking around the cafeteria and caught sight of Cara pretending to be in ecstasy eating a spoonful of yogurt, and of course all her fans were appreciating her wit as usual. The sight of her made me tense right up, so I concentrated on my eggs and bacon, but the next minute I found myself tuning in to a conversation at a table of eighth graders behind me.

"What part are you going for?"

"Well I was going to try for Amy, but Cara Ravenscroft's doing that, so I might try for Meg…"

The name *Cara* was beginning to get on my nerves. Everyone talked about her as though she'd just won an Oscar. I bit my lip. Well, *I* wasn't going to change my mind about Amy. No way. But maybe I ought to have a second choice of role in mind, like Miss Pritchard had suggested. I like the character of Aunt March, because she's feisty and strong, even though she's pretty old. Maybe I'd have Aunt March as my second choice, and then I wouldn't be quite so disappointed if Cara got the role of Amy. I shivered at the thought of that happening and knew I was kidding myself. I'd be gutted if she got the part and I didn't, so I'd just have to work and work at preparing for the audition to make sure that didn't happen. I kept reminding myself about all the main parts I'd had at elementary school, and then there was the time when I acted in a local pantomime with the amateur drama society. There were only five children in it and they'd chosen us out of about twenty, so I *must* be good, mustn't I?

In the end I told Jess not to worry about making

up an excuse for the math teacher.

"Just save me a seat. I'll do it myself," I told her. "In fact, if I really rush I won't even be late."

But I was. In fact I was nearly ten minutes late and I was also in a very bad mood because *Little Women* wasn't in the library. I'd looked it up on the computer to make sure that there definitely was a copy, and there was, which meant that someone had checked it out.

"Sorry I'm late, Mr. Ledbetter. You see, there was a hole in my tights that was growing so fast I thought I might finish up with more runner than tight," I explained as I flopped into my seat next to Jess.

The rest of the class found my excuse hilarious because they all cracked up and one or two gave me a thumbs up, which means, *Thanks for injecting some fun into this boring class.* Mr. Ledbetter was not amused, however.

"Other people might appreciate your acerbic wit, Georgie, but I don't. What you fail to realize is that missing work is not doing you any favors." He looked at me over his glasses. "Christmas vacation is looming and I'm sure you don't want a bad report card."

It was true my dad would blow a fuse if I had a bad report card, because my parents could just barely afford to send me to this school and I was supposed to be working hard and getting myself a good education. That's all Dad ever talks about. So half my brain was making big resolutions about turning over new leaves and concentrating harder in classes, but the other part was wondering what acerbic meant and whether or not it was a good thing. I watched Mr. Ledbetter tapping the interactive whiteboard with a stern look on his face, and decided it might not be the best time to ask him.

After lunch I went to test Mia on her scales. She's doing her seventh grade piano exam in a few weeks, which shows what an incredibly talented musician she is. We were in a little practice room and I had the list of scales in front of me. I love pretending I'm the examiner, reading out all the technical-sounding words.

"Chromatic in contrary motion from C and E please, Miss Roberts."

Mia giggled. "Just say the scale, Georgie. You don't need to say 'Miss Roberts' every time."

When we'd done about fifteen, Mia said she was going to move on to her pieces, so I went out into the hall to practice the Amy speech I'd chosen. Later, I went back into the practice room and Mia pretended to be Miss Pritchard listening to me saying it again.

"It sounds great to me!" she said when I'd finished. "I'd give you the part any day!"

I was over the moon because Mia looked really impressed, but she brought me down to earth with her next words. "What's your second choice of part, Georgie?"

"Um...I thought I'd try Aunt March..."

"Is that a smaller part?"

"Well, it's not *all* that small." Mia was looking at me in a slightly disapproving way so I quickly said, "Not as big as Amy, though."

"All the same," she came straight back, "don't you think you ought to try something slightly smaller? I mean, there'll probably be tons of seventh and eighth graders going for the big parts. Here, let me look."

She started reading through the notes at the front of the script about all the different characters. "What about this one...Hannah the housekeeper? It's a sort of medium-sized role but you'd have to really act like crazy to pretend to be so old and slow, and kind of strict, it says here, yet fond of all the girls..."

I sighed as I took the script back from her. "To be honest, I'm not really interested in being Hannah. Just because I'm only in sixth grade it doesn't mean that I can't have a main role. Miss Pritchard will judge on talent not age." But Mia was frowning and looking anxious so I said something that I knew would please her. "Tell you what, I'll prepare for Amy, Aunt March *and* Hannah, just for you!"

"Do you have time to get all three speeches really good, though?"

"I'll make time. I'll utterly devote myself to them."

And that's exactly what I did over the next two days. As time went on I kept wondering whether or not to tell Mom and Dad that I was going for the part of Amy, but I decided not to because Dad would go off about schoolwork and say that if I had any time to spare I should be working at something important like math or science, instead of learning masses of lines.

In the end I e-mailed home to say that the junior play auditions were coming up and I was going for a small part because all the big parts usually went to eighth graders and I wanted to make sure I had enough time for schoolwork. I thought that was pretty smart of me because now they'd both think I was really fantastic if I got a star part and Dad would be so proud of me that he wouldn't care quite so much if I got a slightly bad report card.

In my heart I thought that the time when Dad stopped worrying so much about my schoolwork would be when the moon turned green, but I tried not to think about that.

Chapter Three

Last class on Thursdays is French. Normally I really enjoy French, even though I'm not much good at it, because I pass the time studying Mam'zelle Clemence's cool accent when she's speaking English, so I can entertain my friends by impersonating her. But today I couldn't concentrate on anything at all except the thought of the auditions that would be starting exactly fifteen minutes after the class finished.

I had my script on my lap so I could keep glancing down at it, but I had to be careful because Mam'zelle Clemence was in a no-nonsense mood and kept us working as a whole class, which made it very difficult to avoid her eagle eye. She was chucking questions at us like confetti and, as usual, I seemed to know less than everyone else in the room.

"Georgie, I'm worrrrrrried about you! Where is your brrrrain? Find eet and use eet!" She wasn't exactly angry but I could tell she was a little exasperated with me. "Stay be-ined at zee end please."

"No I can't!" I blurted out. "It's the auditions at five."

"*A quelle heure alors?*"

"Um...hmm...*cinq heures!*" I managed, with a massive effort.

"Good. You 'ave found your brrrrrain so I weel only keep you for a minute at zee end."

I thought she'd just quickly tell me which pages of the book to look at before the next class, but it turned out to be a mini lecture about not checking my homework before turning it in, and not concentrating hard enough in class. But when she started going through my mistakes from the last assignment I could feel the steam coming out of my ears. Good old Katy came to the rescue though.

"Excuse me, Mam'zelle Clemence, but I've got to go to running club, only I wanted to ask you about costumes for the play and if you thought we might be able to get involved in our fashion club?"

Mam'zelle Clemence absolutely loves fashion so she quickly wished me luck in the auditions, then turned her attention to Katy. I threw Katy a thank-you-for-saving-me look and rushed out at four hundred miles an hour.

Mia was waiting for me, along with Naomi, Grace and Jess, and we shot off to the main building.

"Sure you won't change your mind and audition for a small part at least?" I asked them all. "It would be so much more fun if I had my friends with me at rehearsals." I put on my most pleading face but it didn't do any good.

"I'd rather do detention every day for a week!" Grace said with a shudder, as though I'd asked her to help me slaughter a cow or something. We all laughed because she looked so serious.

I put my hands up. "All right, Grace! No one's forcing you!"

Naomi shook her head. "I really don't like the thought of all those people watching me." That's typical of Naomi. She must be the most modest princess on earth. "But Georgie..." she went on, and I sensed a little lecture coming in my direction. "I know you'll be mega talented and everything, only…try not to be disappointed if you don't get the part you want. It won't be your fault, it's just that if there are two people who are both equally good, I guess Miss Pritchard will choose whoever's older, as that's the fairest thing to do."

She was looking at me really seriously and my heart didn't exactly sink, but it certainly started floundering around because Naomi's always right about stuff like that and if Cara and I both did as well as each other in the auditions, then Miss Pritchard would choose Cara because she's older. The floundering only lasted about two seconds though, because I had a sudden picture of the teachers at my elementary school all congratulating me after the fifth grade play. There was one particularly strict and grumpy teacher who even made a point of coming up to me the next day when she was on playground duty. She said she'd had tears of laughter rolling down her face during the play, because I'd brought the character of Nick Bottom to life in such a comic way. I remember her shaking her head and saying, "You know, I never appreciated how funny Shakespeare was until now!"

Naomi and Grace wished me good luck over and over again and then went rushing off, and Jess said, "Don't forget to find out whether I'm allowed to help paint the scenery," as she followed after them.

When Mia and I got upstairs into the corridor outside the drama hall we found it absolutely bursting with chattering students, and on the door of the drama hall was a large notice.

NO ENTRY UNLESS AUDITIONING!

"I'd better go then," said Mia.

"Yes, I guess…" I looked at my watch. One minute to five. "Help! This is it!" I squeaked and Mia gave me a tight hug.

"Trillions and quadrillions of luck, then, Georgie." Then she lowered her voice. "But don't forget, even if you don't get Amy, it'll be great to get any part with all this bunch here!"

When she said that I suddenly felt more determined than ever to prove what I could do. Huh! My friends would all be eating their words by dinner time. Or was it eating their hats? I'd never been too sure on that one.

As soon as Mia had gone, the drama-hall door opened and Miss Pritchard beckoned the chattering throng inside. I could hear Cara's loud voice behind me but I didn't turn around.

"It's cool the way the singers link up all the scenes, isn't it?" she was saying. "So that we get the idea of time passing without having to act out every little bit of the story."

I felt my hackles rising. I didn't know there were going to be singers in the play. So how come Cara knew? I resisted the temptation to start questioning her about that though, and tried to calm myself down so I'd be in the right kind of mood for the auditions.

"Okay, come and sit down, everyone," said Miss Pritchard, raising her voice above the noise.

When she spoke we all listened, just like we'd done in assembly, and I thought what a powerful lady she is. In fact I decided right there and then that she was going to be my role model. She looked so cool in her trendy sweat pants and white T-shirt, with her hair in a high ponytail.

"Firstly, can I just check that there isn't anyone here who doesn't want to audition?" Glancing around I noticed that Cara only had two friends with her now, so the rest of her fan club had obviously just been waiting outside to support their idol.

"I know it takes a great deal of courage to go up onstage and act in front of your peers," Miss Pritchard went on, "and I could have organized private individual auditions, but this way saves a lot of time and it's helpful for me to be able to see whether or not you're going to be self-conscious when it comes to rehearsing and performing…"

I hadn't actually been worried about everyone watching me, but I knew some people would be, and now Miss Pritchard had made a special point of mentioning it I was determined to show her exactly how confident and unselfconscious I was.

"As you know, the eighth graders have already auditioned for their first choice of part and I've noted down their second choices. I'm going to do exactly the same with you in a few moments, so I'd like you to write down your name and your second choice, if you've got one, on this paper. If you don't manage to get a speaking part this time, there's always next year, remember. Just one more point… the stage in this hall is much smaller than the one in the theater, so bear that in mind. Okay, when I call out the name of a character, if you want to audition for that character for your first choice you should come and wait at the front and I'll send you up one at a time. Any questions?"

"When will we find out if we've got a part?" someone asked.

"I'll get the list up by morning break tomorrow hopefully, or definitely by lunchtime. Okay!" Miss

Pritchard rubbed her hands together and gave us a great big grin as though she was really excited. Then she went and sat down at her desk with a notepad in front of her. "Let's start with the part of Meg."

I was really surprised when only one girl went up, but then I realized that actually it wasn't all that surprising because Meg is the oldest of the March sisters so most people probably thought Miss Pritchard would cast an eighth grader in that role. The girl auditioning seemed really nervous. Her voice sounded so shaky in the silent hall that Miss Pritchard stopped her right in the middle and said, "Don't worry, Adelaide. I know it's terrible being first, but I'll give you a little tip. Whenever you're faced with a crowd of people staring at you, just pretend they're stark naked, then you won't feel nervous at all!" Immediately everyone cracked up laughing, including Adelaide, and from then on everything felt more relaxed.

By the time the auditions for Jo, Mrs. March, Aunt March and the grandfather had been done, I was positively tingling with excitement, because I knew I could make my voice come out louder than anyone had so far, and it was obvious Miss Pritchard had told us about the stage in the theater being much bigger than this one because she wanted us to speak up. I lost count of the number of times my teachers at elementary school had gotten me to demonstrate my great big voice, as they called it, for people who were too quiet. "Georgie can project her voice so well," they used to say.

I also secretly thought that no one was putting enough expression into their voice, which made them sound flat and boring. I guess Miss Pritchard was thinking the same thing, because a few times she reminded us to really think hard about how the characters must be feeling and try to put that across as we spoke.

She made at least one comment after each audition. Sometimes it was about relaxing or not being too stiff or using your eyes, and sometimes it was a word of praise or a suggestion about what your second choice should be. I'd written Aunt March as my second choice on the clipboard sheet, but there wasn't room for any third choices, which was a little annoying when I'd gone to the trouble to learn Amy, Aunt March *and* Hannah the housekeeper. I noticed that Cara had written Beth as her second choice, so now I was really hoping that if I did a totally great audition I'd get to be Amy, and maybe she'd be Beth.

There were four seventh graders auditioning for

Beth and I noticed that Cara scarcely bothered to watch them. That must have meant that she wasn't impressed, even though they were all good, I thought. My mouth started to go dry then because I guessed it would be the part of Amy next, so I licked my lips and swallowed once or twice. But then another teacher came into the hall to have a word with Miss Pritchard and while they were talking, all the students started chatting.

"You were really good last year, Cara," someone said, which made my ears prick up.

"Thanks."

Cara didn't actually sound at all grateful for the compliment.

"What part are you auditioning for this time?" was the next question.

"Amy."

"Well, you certainly look like her!" the girl said, and when I glanced sideways I saw Cara run her fingers through her hair.

"That's what my friends keep saying."

"Okay, back to business!" Miss Pritchard clapped her hands for silence. "Let's have anyone who wants to try for the part of Amy next, please."

My heart raced as I walked to the front behind Cara's bobbing blonde curls, and suddenly I felt really scared. From the back, Cara looked so much like the picture on my book that it just seemed obvious she'd get the part.

When I got to the front I realized that Cara and I were the only two standing there.

"Cara, we'll let...sorry...um...what's your name?"

"Georgie Henderson."

Miss Pritchard gave me a nice bright smile. "We'll let Georgie go first."

I didn't look at Cara, just went up onto the stage and waited for my cue to start.

"No script! Excellent!" Miss Pritchard commented, which made me feel very proud as I was only the third person to audition without a script. I've always been good at learning lines and I'd managed to memorize the whole speech.

I took a deep breath and began. As soon as the first words came out of my mouth I felt as though I really was Amy, all confident and a bit stressy. I thought I could feel Miss Pritchard's eyes on me too, and I hoped she was pleased that I wasn't acting woodenly. I threw my voice as far as I possibly could to show it wouldn't get lost in the big theater. No way could anyone accuse me of not speaking loudly enough for the people in the back row of the audience. When I'd finished I felt on top of the world and saw that Miss Pritchard was smiling, which was a good sign.

"Thank you, Georgie. You're certainly excellent at projecting your voice, but the stage is amplified in the new theater so there's no need to force it or to overact in any way."

I froze. This was terrible. Then I heard the smallest of snickers, which Miss Pritchard couldn't possibly have heard from where she was sitting, and when I made the mistake of glancing at Cara I saw she was rolling her eyes at her friends.

"What did you write down for your second choice, Georgie?" Miss Pritchard continued brightly.

A horrible sinking feeling seemed to be dragging my spirits down to my shoes and gluing my feet to the floor.

"I put Aunt March, but—"

"Aunt March! That's interesting. I think I can see why you chose that..."

"Yes, but—"

"Aunt March is a particularly popular role it seems. Quite a few eighth graders are interested in it..." She tipped her head to the side. "But, you know, I'm thinking you might be good at the role of Amy's larger-than-life school friend, Susie Perkins, who's got a few words at the beginning of the play."

I just stared at her. I couldn't believe what I was hearing. My sinking feeling disappeared in a flash and I felt absolutely furious. What an insult! Nobody's ever accused me of overacting or forcing my voice, and I wasn't interested in the part of Amy's school friend. I couldn't even remember that character from the book. I wanted to be Amy herself.

"I didn't know the stage in the theater was going to be amplified," I said, trying not to sound sulky. "Couldn't I try the speech again?"

"I'm sorry, Georgie, there isn't time. And even with a quieter delivery, you still wouldn't be quite right for the role. Amy is...certainly exuberant, but in a more subtle, refined way. She has a will of her own but she's not completely...sure of herself. Think about Susie Perkins and write it down if you'd like to be considered for that role, all right?" She smiled brightly and tapped the piece of paper that people had written their second choices on. I was desperate to mention about Hannah being my third choice but she'd clearly finished with me. "Cara, would you like to go up?"

There was only one set of steps to the stage so

Cara and I had to pass each other. I don't know whether she was looking at me because I stared at the ground. My whole body was trembling, not with disappointment, but with anger. How was I supposed to know that the theater stage was amplified? I'm not a mind-reader. Why did she tell us about the stage being bigger if she didn't want us to project our voices? I felt like marching straight out of the hall, but I was too curious about Cara's acting to leave without seeing it. Her friends were standing not far in front of me and I saw them whisper to each other behind their hands, and then turn around and look at me as though I was pathetic. Huh! How would they like it if I snickered and smirked during *their* auditions. Some people are so mean.

"When you're ready." I saw Miss Pritchard sit up straighter and lean forward.

I swallowed as Cara began. She didn't have a script either and the words just seemed to dance out of her mouth without any effort. She was doing a different speech from the one I'd done. It was a part where Amy was supposed to be practically laughing, and I had to admit it was good the way Cara got the words out while seeming to laugh at the same time. Even so, it was pretty quiet. I could only just hear her from the back and she didn't move around very much, just used her shoulders and head and eyes. Then suddenly she'd finished and the hall was filled with clapping. Everyone had burst into applause. Cara pretended to be embarrassed but then she practically skipped down the stairs and rushed over to her friends, who all patted her on the back and gave her hugs and told her how fantastic she was. Miss Pritchard was engrossed in writing on her notepad, so the room was full of chatter again.

"Whew! Thank goodness that's over!" said Cara, pretending to be exhausted as she smiled around at everyone. Her eyes caught mine and I saw a little mocking gleam in them.

"Aren't you going to change your second choice to Susie Perkins, Georgie? I agree with Miss Pritchard, you'd be good at that."

One or two of her friends turned away as though they were trying to hide their amusement, and it suddenly struck me that Cara was being sarcastic. My blood boiled. She didn't care about my feelings at all. She just wanted to put me down and make me look a fool.

"No way am I changing my second choice," I said in a hiss. "Why would I want the stupid Susie Perkins part when I'm easily good enough for Amy?

How was I supposed to know that the stage is amplified?" I snapped.

She glared at me then. "Well no one else got up there and yelled out the words, did they?"

The fury inside me was bubbling.

"But if the stage *wasn't* amplified, *they* wouldn't have been heard at the back."

Cara's face turned into one big sneer then. "It's not a pantomime, Georgie. It's not all about loud voices and great big gestures, you know." Then she tossed her stupid yellow curls and stalked off.

So did I. Right out of the building.

Chapter Four

All the way back to Hazeldean I talked myself into a red-hot temper. *Great big gestures.* Huh! What nerve! Cara made me sick. I did *not* do great big gestures… They were only small… Well okay, *pretty big*, but that's because you have to exaggerate things on the stage. It's not like acting in a movie. You can't be subtle or the audience won't get it. And why weren't we told before about the stage being amplified? It's not fair on the sixth graders. And especially not fair on me. I went to loads of trouble to learn all my lines, *and* I learned all Aunt March's and Hannah's lines, just in case… But Susie Perkins.

Susie Perkins! I yanked the script out of my bag to see how many lines Susie Perkins actually had. Then I rammed it straight back in again because I decided I didn't care. I knew it was a pathetic little part and there was no way I was going to settle for that. In fact I didn't want anything more to do with the whole stupid play. Cara Ravenscroft could go and stuff herself and so could Miss Pritchard. More subtle and refined, really!

I crashed through the Hazeldean front door and went to find Mia. I expected her to be in one of the practice rooms but she wasn't, and it made me even madder that I had to walk all around the stupid boarding house looking for her. Eventually I realized she must be in the dorm. My legs ached by the time I'd climbed the steps to the third floor, where our dorm is, and I felt too angry to speak to anyone. I shoved open the door and scarcely looked to the left or right, just catching glimpses of Mia, Grace and Jess at their desks. Then I climbed up to my bed and flopped onto it, closing my eyes.

For a few seconds there wasn't a sound and I suddenly thought that maybe I'd imagined seeing Mia and the other two. Perhaps I was so overcome with anger that I'd totally lost my mind and I was seeing ghosts. But a second later Mia coughed.

"Oh no...Georgie..." she said softly.

Mia knows me better than anyone and she was able to see instantly that something was badly wrong.

"Wh...what...exactly...happened?" Grace asked in the same quiet voice.

I sat up like a jack-in-the-box and felt my rage bubbling up all over again. "I'll tell you what happened. What happened was that Cara was always going to get whatever role she went for because Miss Pritchard thinks she's the best actress in the world, just like everyone else in her fan club does. And loads of people didn't speak up or use enough expression or anything. But *I* was told that I was speaking too loudly because it turns out that the stage in the stupid theater is amplified and if I'd known that then *obviously* I wouldn't have done it so loudly. And when I said that to the big Oscar-winning Cara Ravenscroft afterward, she just said, 'It's not a pantomime, you know!' And I honestly wish I hadn't spent so long learning all those lines. The whole thing's just so totally unfair and I don't want any more to do with it. The end!"

There was another silence, except that we could probably all still hear those last two words of mine hanging in the air. They sounded stupid. I wish I hadn't said them. But I didn't regret anything else I'd said.

I flopped back down again and the next minute Mia was sitting beside me. "Oh, poor, poor Georgie! That was really cruel of Cara to say that."

I looked at the wall because I didn't feel like seeing Mia's sympathetic eyes. I knew it'd make me too sad.

"But did Miss Pritchard actually say that Cara had definitely gotten the part?" asked Jess.

"No, but it's obvious she does."

"Was there anyone else auditioning for Amy apart from you two?" asked Mia.

"No."

"Well then, you might still be in with a chance," said Jess.

"Did you do it as well as you did it for me?" asked Mia.

They just didn't get it, and it was making me even angrier. "Look, I told you, I never stood a chance against Cara!"

"But even if you don't get Amy, you'll get Aunt March or Hannah, I expect," said Mia, in her cheeriest voice, and I realized I still had to explain about Poo-sie Perkins, only I absolutely did not feel like it right then.

Naomi and Katy came in at that moment and I groaned and buried my head in the pillow.

"How did you do?" they shrieked, but I guess Mia or one of the others must have signaled to them that it wasn't a good question to be asking because the dorm was suddenly embarrassingly silent. Then after a moment it filled up with false-sounding chatter, and Mia gave my shoulder a quick pat before climbing down from my bed, which made me feel like a dog.

I spent the rest of the evening wishing that this day would hurry up and be over. I just couldn't stop thinking about the auditions, and every time I pictured Cara's face sneering at me or heard Miss Pritchard's voice saying those awful words to me, I filled up with anger, which made it impossible to concentrate on homework or even TV. I think dinner was the worst time of all because I had to suffer the sight of Cara, still showing off with all her friends. Even though she was at a table on the other side of the cafeteria from where we were all sitting, I could tell she was making sure she was the center of attention the whole time by the way she talked more than anyone else and kept tossing her head and running her fingers through her hair.

"Forget about Cara," said Naomi, following my eyes. "She's just not worth worrying about."

And I tried. I really tried.

Waking up the following morning was absolutely terrible. I was still as angry as ever. But the anger was heavier because it was mixed with sadness. This was the day when Miss Pritchard was going to put the list up and everyone who'd auditioned would find out how they'd done. I was just wondering whether there was any chance at all that my friends might forget about the whole subject of the play, when Mia shook my shoulder.

"Come on, Georgie! Get up! You should be excited. You'll find out what part you got today!"

This time when I thought back to the auditions I just felt flat. There was no way I'd get a part because I hadn't changed my second choice to Susie Perkins, and Miss Pritchard would have said if she'd thought I'd be good at any other part.

"I won't get a part," I said firmly.

"Let's go and look at break time, shall we?" said Naomi, as though I hadn't spoken.

I didn't mean to sound horrible but the last thing I wanted was for my friends to know how useless

I was and all feel sorry for me. "What do you mean 'we'? I'll go on my own, okay?"

"Are you sure?" asked Mia gently.

I nodded, trying to ignore the hurt look on her face, and went off to the bathroom.

English was the first class of the day, which is one of my better subjects because the teacher makes everything really interesting and we sometimes get to act out parts of plays or read a poem or a short story out loud. There was no way I could have read anything out loud this morning, not after what happened yesterday. Anyway, I was too tense about the thought of the cast list going up. But the English class was okay because we plotted stories in pairs, and Mia came up with most of the ideas. After English it was math. I don't think I took in a single fact in that math class, which wasn't going to do me any favors when it came to homework that night, and neither would it help my grades. At the back of my mind I was starting to dread showing Mom and Dad my report card, but only at the very back. The rest of my mind was taken up with thoughts of the play.

When the bell rang for morning break, my heart started racing. Mia and the others walked up to the main building with me then waited outside while I went in. Lots of eighth graders were standing in front of the noticeboard, all talking excitedly and prodding the list. I couldn't bring myself to look with so many people there, so I faked a big interest in the photos on the opposite wall and waited till the eighth graders had started to drift away. Then I turned around just as Cara and her fan club appeared. There was nowhere to escape to, apart from the drama hall, but even that was impossible because I could see from looking through the glass panels at the top of the door that something was going on in there. So I started studying the photos again and hoped that everyone would be so taken up with the list of parts that no one would spot me.

"Yes, you've got it! Congratulations!" said one of Cara's friends. And my blood ran cold.

"Thanks," said Cara coolly.

After that they talked about the small parts that Cara's friends had gotten. Then there was a sudden flurry of whispers and I realized they must have finally noticed me, so I turned around wearing my most laid-back expression and found them all staring at me.

"Congratulations, Cara!" I said in a fake voice, and then I made for the door, as though my mission at the photograph noticeboard was complete.

"Your name isn't on the list at all," Cara came straight back at me, which felt like a stab in the stomach. "Don't you wish you'd gone for the part of Susie Perkins?" she added.

"No I don't!" I snapped, wishing she'd get off my case. It was like she was still trying to rub it in.

"But don't you even want to know who did get the part?" she went on.

"Why should I be interested in that?" I asked coldly.

"Because it's obvious you didn't come up here to look at photos," she sneered, which naturally made her friends laugh. "Anyway, it was Jemima Langton."

"Jemima Langton," I repeated. "At least she's not a show-off like some people."

Cara's eyes flashed with fury. "Huh! I like that! If anyone's a show-off around here it's you, Georgie Henderson!" She tossed her head and walked off. "Come on, you guys."

By then the whole bottom had dropped out of my world and nothing seemed to matter anymore. I wandered toward the list and pretended to be scanning it in a bored kind of way, just in case Cara was still hanging around. Really, though, I was scouring it carefully to see if Cara had missed my name by any miracle. It didn't take a minute to see that she hadn't. The last tiny little ray of hope had vanished and I was hurting so much that I don't know how I managed to get out of the building without crying.

"Oh no!" said Mia when she saw my face. And I could tell she was genuinely shocked.

"I told you," I said in a thin voice. But then just when I thought I was about to burst into tears, because all my friends were saying, "Poor Georgie" and "Never mind," I suddenly felt another wave of anger building up inside me.

"It's so unfair!" I practically spat. "And I can't stand the way Cara is all gloaty because she's got the part I wanted."

"But did you get...Hannah...or anything?" Mia asked gently.

I looked down and pretended to be absorbed in drawing the wrinkles up out of my tights. "Nah. I told you I wouldn't." I had to straighten up eventually and the moment I did, Mia put her arm around me.

"If only you'd known about the theater stage being amplified, Georgie..."

A horrible sadness sunk into me and I stayed as rigid as I could, wishing Mia would take her arm away because it wasn't helping me to be strong and that seemed like the most important thing at the moment.

"At least you've got…next year *and* the next," said Grace. Why were they all speaking in such soft voices?

"I'm okay about it, honestly," I managed to say.

There was another little silence, then Jess spoke. "Why don't you join art club? We're starting to paint the set next week."

Katy's eyes lit up. "Or you could join fashion club. I ran into Mam'zelle Clemence just now and she says there are lots of costumes in the wardrobe department but they need more, and we're designing them and choosing the fabrics in fashion club."

"I didn't even know there was a wardrobe department," I said, making a huge effort to act as normally as possible, even though I could feel my strength draining away. "Where is it?"

"Upstairs in the main building," said Katy. "Right at the very top. Apparently there's a little narrow staircase that leads to a loft and there are rails and rails of clothes tucked away in there."

"We should go and see it!" said Naomi, brightly.

I hated their happiness. It seemed so fake. And I didn't need their sympathy. It was like they were trying to root out my shame, and I wouldn't let them. I just wanted everyone to forget about the play and everything to do with it. I shrugged a doesn't-bother-me-either-way shrug which juddered Mia's arm off my shoulder, and the moment I'd done it I wanted to take it back because I suddenly felt more alone than I'd ever felt.

"I'm pretty fed up with the subject of plays to be honest," I managed to say. "I'm...going to the bathroom."

I walked fast, my head still spinning with thoughts and feelings. I hated knowing that Cara had gotten the part of Amy and I hadn't gotten a part at all. I hated it so much that I felt sick and wished I could wake up and find the whole thing had all been a terrible dream. I didn't go the bathroom. I just walked down to the athletics field and on the way I switched on my phone and found two messages. One was from my grandma and the other was from Mom. I read Mom's first.

Gr8 news bout play. Did u get a part?
If so let us no ASAP cos dad away
4 work from Dec 13th 2 16th. but still
time to alter it. luv u. M X

Oh well, at least Dad wouldn't have to rearrange his business trip. I read Grandma's text next...

So excited about the play, darling.
Wild horses would not keep me away!
Love Gran

Grandma's message must have taken her ages to write. She's so slow at texting and hasn't gotten the hang of shortening words. A rock of despair seemed to drop into the pit of my stomach. She was just assuming I'd get a part. My selfish behavior was letting everyone down. How was I ever going to explain to poor Grandma that I wasn't actually in the play, and that it was my own fault? I couldn't tell my family about turning my nose up at the Susie Perkins part, any more than I could admit it to my friends. There wasn't one single good thing about the mess I was in. I'd thought I didn't want anything to do with the play just because I couldn't get what I wanted, and now I was paying for my stupid hot-headed behavior. Oh well, Dad would be pleased that the play rehearsals weren't taking any time away from my schoolwork, so at least I might be able to try and improve my grades before the Christmas break. I quickly texted the same reply to Mom and Grandma.

Only tiny parts 4 6th graders.
Lots of hangin around
at rehursals so didn't aud.
Luv G x

I closed my eyes and slowly opened them again. I felt weighed down with sadness and shame. I stopped walking and stared down at my feet.

Something had changed. I wasn't angry with Cara or her friends or Miss Pritchard anymore. Well, I was still angry with Cara, but most of all I was angry with myself. I shouldn't have gone flying off the handle at the auditions. Mom and Dad are always telling me I'm far too impulsive. I should have been sensible and written down Susie Perkins as my second choice. What an idiot I was. And now it was too late. There was nothing I could do.

Chapter Five

The math homework was impossible. I tried to get Jess to help me but she didn't have any more clue than I did, and in the end she went to the front to tell Miss Fosbrook, who was on duty. Miss Fosbrook is the assistant dorm mom and she's such a nice person that she practically did the whole assignment for Jess and me, which meant that I didn't need to concentrate at all. I knew this wasn't helping me in the long run and I didn't like the picture that came into my mind of Dad's angry face reading my terrible report card, but I quickly shook it away.

And then my mind filled up with thoughts about the play, just like it did all the time now. I'd tried so hard to forget about it, but I simply couldn't. I was too curious. I'd started wondering exactly how *Castles in the Air* was going to be different from *Little Women.* The little mini-scripts hadn't given me any clues. I only knew what Cara had said about singers linking the action and helping the story to move forward, so now I wanted to know which parts of the story would be shown in song. If only I could get a hold of a copy of *Little Women* I could try and figure it out. It was true that so far I hadn't exactly had much success with finding *Little Women*, but then I hadn't tried the massive main school library yet.

As soon as I'd had that thought I couldn't let it go. It grew and grew inside my head until it was the most important thing in my life, because that's what I'm like. I can't help it. I looked at my watch and willed the time till study hour finished to go faster because I planned to whip over to the library at eight thirty on the dot. I'd be breaking the rules because we're all supposed to be in our dorms after eight thirty during the week, but no one would miss me for a few minutes. The book was almost sure to be there. I didn't want Mia and the others to know that I was reading *Little Women* though, or they'd realize I was still all wrapped up with the play and start being all sympathetic again, which was the last thing I needed when I was trying to hide my stupid rashness from them.

"Just going to get some fresh air," I announced casually, the moment Miss Fosbrook said we could go.

"What!" laughed Jess. "Are you sure you're feeling okay, Georgie? You don't normally notice the difference between fresh air and any other sort of air."

"But it's nearly eight thirty," said Mia.

"It's okay, I'm not going anywhere much. It's just that I've got a headache from all the math."

Mia immediately offered to take me to Miss Jennings, so I had to say I was fine apart from needing to clear my head after the strenuous math homework. Of course that made everyone laugh, which felt nice and normal and back to how we always were. But then that good feeling was spoiled because as I was going out I distinctly heard Jess whisper that she thought I was up to something. So now I'd have to move extra fast, especially as the library was all the way at the other end of school and the premises are so enormous. I also had to be careful not to draw attention to myself, because of the strict rule about sixth graders being in their own boarding houses after eight thirty.

Even though there are lots of lamps all over the place at Silver Spires, it still felt dark outside, and because of my big imagination I could see plenty of spooky things hidden in trees and lurking around the side of the boarding houses. It would have been nice to flop into one of the squishy beanbags in the common room and watch something funny on TV for half an hour before bed, and yet here I was scaring myself on a long dark trek to the school library just to get a book. If anyone had told me a few days ago that I'd be doing this now, I simply wouldn't have believed them. Something weird had happened to me because of that stupid play. It had cast a spell on me, that was clinging like sticky cobweb threads that I couldn't peel off.

It felt strange switching on the library light. The school feels so different at nighttime. *Okay, quick, Georgie! Find the book. Who wrote* Little Women? *Louisa M. Alcott.* I went straight to the As and ran my finger slowly along until the Bs started. This was unbelievable. It *had* to be here. So I went back to the start and looked carefully at every single spine until I knew for sure, with big sinking certainty, that there wasn't a single copy.

Wandering back to Hazeldean I couldn't care less whether there was a gang of spooks ready to jump out at me from one of the trees and rip me to pieces. Nothing was going right in my life. Nothing. I went into Hazeldean and saw that the clock said just gone four minutes to nine. Even that didn't make me speed up. What was a little telling-off? I trudged up the three flights of stairs slowly and heavily with my head down, then paused outside our dorm to look at the notice on the door. I'd put it there myself at the beginning of the school year…

Katy the Queen of Style
Grace the Sportswoman
Jess the Artist
Mia the Musician
Naomi the Wise One
Georgie the Actress

Huh! What nonsense. I wasn't an actress. It ought to say, *Georgie the Loser*.

"It's almost nine! Where have you been?" Mia asked me the very second I opened the door.

"Just walking around."

"But I went out to look for you and you weren't anywhere."

I didn't answer because the tiniest ray of hope had just popped up from nowhere. Maybe the copy of *Little Women* from the Hazeldean library had been returned.

"See you in a sec."

"You've forgotten your washbag!"

"Oh yeah." I grabbed my washbag and towel and raced off downstairs.

"Where are you off to, Georgie Henderson? Bed! Now!" Miss Jennings was leaning over the banister, and although there wasn't an actual echo it still felt as though those cross words of hers were bouncing off the walls of the stairwell. Maybe I did care about getting a telling-off, after all, because my skin had gone a little goosebumpy.

"I've left my book in the common room. Please, please, please let me get it, oh kind Miss Jennings!" I did praying hands and tilted my face up with my eyes closed.

"Go on then, and make it snappy!"

"Thank you!" I definitely caught a glimmer of a smile on Miss Jennings's face when I opened my eyes, and it cheered me up a bit.

I went into the common room willing the book to be there. And it was.

"Yessss!" I told the empty room, as I hid it

under my towel and scrambled off to the bathroom.

"Has your headache gone away?" asked Mia when I went back into the dorm a few minutes later. "You seem better all of a sudden."

"Yep!" I replied chirpily, as I quickly got into my jammies and snuggled up in bed. I was aware of the others looking at each other, but no one said anything else.

We're allowed to read with our little individual night-lights on till nine thirty, then whoever's on duty comes and checks that all lights are out. My friends didn't ask me what I was reading, thank goodness, because I didn't want to have to lie to them and there was no way I was admitting it was *Little Women*. As soon as Miss Jennings had done her lights-out check, I got my key-ring flashlight and tried it out under the covers, but it was useless. I couldn't see a thing and had to wait till I was pretty sure everyone was asleep before switching my night-light back on. That was a really frustrating wait, I can tell you. Nobody pounced on me to switch the light off, thank goodness, which meant they were all asleep, and at last I was free to read to my heart's content. I snuggled into the deepest, most comfortable part of the bed and buried myself in the book, reading and reading until I couldn't keep my eyes open anymore.

Good old Katy had proved the great Cara Ravenscroft wrong because Mrs. Chambers was very happy to have help with costumes from a sixth grade student, and Katy couldn't wait to get started.

"What era is *Little Women* set in, Georgie?" she asked me one lunchtime, as we were waiting to return our trays. "Would they have worn long dresses, or what?"

I loved explaining about the clothing, especially as I was so into the book by then. "Well the dresses would be gathered in at the waist, then flowing down to the ground with ruff necks and puffed sleeves for the younger sisters and maybe floaty sleeves for the older ones."

I was so deep into our conversation that I never noticed Cara right in front of me with her tray until she turned around. For what felt like a minute, but was probably only a second, we just stared at each other coldly. Then she swung back around again.

"What's going on between Cara and you?" Mia asked in an accusing tone, as soon as we were out of the hall. "You're not still upset with her about the play, surely?"

"Yes I told you...she was horrible to me after the auditions so why should I act friendly to her?" I said coolly.

Mia frowned and the others looked down. At that moment I wished there was no such person as Cara Ravenscroft. She obviously hated my guts for accusing her of being a show-off. And as for what I felt about her...well it wasn't exactly hate, but every time I saw her all my feelings of shame and regret came rushing back to the surface, putting me in a terrible mood.

The more I tried to avoid Cara the more she kept popping up everywhere, which was really starting to bug me. We always gave each other the most horrible look and it had grown into somewhat of a competition to see who could stare the other one out, which usually finished in her rolling her eyes and looking away with a sneer on her face. But there was another reason I didn't want to see her. I was starting to panic that she might spill the beans to my friends about what had really happened at the auditions and how I'd refused the smaller part. The only time I could relax was during the weekend, because I could be sure I wouldn't see Cara. On Saturday afternoons and Sundays there are almost always different activities for the various grades, and in between times students usually hang out in their own boarding houses. All our boarding houses are named after trees. Hazeldean is the best, of course, and Cara's is Beech House, which is all the way over on the other side of school, thank goodness. As soon as Monday came I would feel myself tensing up again, because I knew I was much more likely to pass her in the cafeteria or a hallway or somewhere, but we just kept on giving each other evil stares.

"I don't get what this big feud between you and Cara is all about," Mia said, one time. Her eyes had had the same look in them as when she's feeling homesick. "I can understand that you don't like her because she's been so horrible, but why does *she* have a problem with *you*?"

I put my arm around Mia because I don't like it when she's sad. "I'm just ignoring her...so she's ignoring me back. That's all."

"Well, why don't *you* be the sensible, mature one and talk to her one day," suggested Naomi. "Then she'll realize how stupid she's being. Or do you want *me* to have a word with her?" she added.

"No!" I must have spoken very loudly because

everyone seemed to jump about half a mile into the air.

"Okay!" said Naomi, putting her hands up and eyeing me warily, as though I was a bull about to charge at her.

I went for my calmest tones then. "I'm sure she'll come around at some point, and I really don't feel like making friends yet, so promise me you won't say anything, okay?"

Naomi nodded slowly but I could feel her eyes boring into mine, like she was trying to see inside my head and find out what was going on in there. She would have had a shock if she'd been able to read my mind, I can tell you, because it was bursting with pictures from *Little Women*. I'd read the whole book twice and the second time I'd tried to visualize every chapter as a scene in *Castles in the Air*, so now I was absolutely desperate to find out whether my imaginings were right. A plan started to take shape in my head, and one afternoon at the end of school I carried it out.

As soon as the others had gone to clubs, and Mia had gone to choir, I made my way to the new theater and stood outside the door for ages trying to hear what was going on inside. I didn't dare go in because everyone would turn and stare and Miss Pritchard would probably send me away. So instead, I went upstairs and crept in through the back door at the top of the tiered seating area that looks down onto the stage. No one looked up, because they were so absorbed in what they were doing, and even if they had they probably wouldn't have seen me because I stayed all the way at the back where there were no house lights and it was really dark.

I'd never been up here before. It felt magic and I sat there for a whole hour and a half just staring down, watching the play taking shape. It was the best hour and a half I'd had in ages. All my feelings against Miss Pritchard fizzled away because I had to admit she was a wonderful director. She stopped the action loads of times to make comments about the way someone was saying a line, or to alter people's positions onstage or something. The part that was being rehearsed was the one near the beginning of the story with Susie Perkins in it. My eyes were on stalks.

"Just relax when you walk to the front, Jemima," said Miss Pritchard. "Saunter with a bit of a swagger, like this, and toss your head. Then, when you suddenly freeze in fear, it'll be much funnier because of the contrast."

I knew exactly what Miss Pritchard meant and

I felt a massive jolt of jealousy that it wasn't me down there playing the part of Susie. I thought the general standard of acting was easily as good as some of the teenage actors I'd seen on TV, though, and that was because Miss Pritchard was just the best director. I couldn't wait till eighth grade when she'd be teaching *me*.

My eyes were glued to Cara whenever she was onstage. I so wanted her to be terrible and I was dying for her to mess up and for Miss Pritchard to have words with her. But she didn't mess up, and I realized with a horrible dull aching feeling that it was true what everyone said. She *was* one of the best actresses on that stage. A girl named Rebecca, who was playing the part of Meg, kept forgetting her words, and at one point Miss Pritchard suddenly went nuts, and slapped her script against the grand piano, demanding to know why Rebecca still hadn't learned her lines. I had to stifle my gasp of shock, and shrank down in my seat, watching in amazement as the whole cast seemed to melt away till there was only Rebecca left out in the open, going red and stammering that she was sorry.

"I should think so too! It strikes me that you're only semi-committed to this play. I want this scene word-perfect for tomorrow's rehearsal."

But as soon as she'd finished blowing her top, Miss Pritchard was back to her calm self again and the rehearsal went on.

Usually, time only whizzes by when I'm watching a really good program on TV, but this rehearsal gripped me so much that ninety minutes honestly felt like twenty, and I couldn't wait to come back the next day. The problem was, the next day seemed so far away. There was dinner and homework and a whole night and assembly and a ton of boring classes to get through first. How was I going to bear it? I didn't want to let go of the magic that the play was weaving in my mind, not even for a second, and I knew there was only one way to hold onto it. I'd been watching some sixth graders who'd been sitting in the front row all through the rehearsal and hadn't been onstage a single time. Miss Pritchard had praised them for being so patient, and promised them she'd be doing their scene next time. They all had copies of the play that they'd rolled up into tubes and tucked into the sides of their seats. Never once during the rehearsal had they followed the play on their scripts, though, and they probably didn't even need them if they were only in the crowd scenes. So it wouldn't matter if one went missing, would it?

As the rehearsal drew to a close I started trying to hypnotize them by staring hard at the backs of their heads, willing them to forget about the scripts and walk out of the theater without a backward glance. I kept it up for a good minute until Miss Pritchard suddenly announced that the rehearsal was over and that anyone not knowing their lines next time would risk getting chucked off the play. I had to duck down at that point to make sure no one saw me, but my heart started to beat a little faster at those words of hers, because if someone did get chucked off the play, it might turn out to be just the break I needed, except that Cara was totally word-perfect, so there was no chance of getting the part I really wanted. All the same, I'd be happy to have any part now, even if it was the smallest one in the whole play. It would just be so good to feel a part of what was going on, instead of being a little insignificant person watching in secret from the darkest corner of the auditorium.

The moment everyone had gone I leaped down to the front, praying that I'd find a script somewhere, anywhere, among the seats, but incredibly there wasn't a single one. My eyes scanned the whole theater, just in case, and bingo! I spotted a tattered one just inside the wings. I grabbed it, then ducked out of sight faster than you could say *Georgie Henderson*, because someone had come back into the theater. I inched back into the wings, but not before I'd seen that it was Rebecca. A second later her footsteps were approaching my hiding place, so I had to shrink further back and found myself in a dark corridor. I crept along it with absolutely no idea where I was going because I'd never been backstage before. There were rooms going off on either side which I realized were dressing rooms.

At the far end of the corridor there was a little recess, where I waited out of sight, looking for places in my uniform where I could tuck the script so it wouldn't be noticed. Then I'd simply be able to walk out and it wouldn't matter who saw me. But the Silver Spires uniform clearly wasn't designed for concealing vast wads of paper, so I just had to wait until I thought the coast might be clear. I knew I should have gone out of the backstage door, which was only a few yards away from where I was hiding, but first I wanted to see what it felt like to make an entrance onto the stage from the wings.

I tiptoed back and poked my head around. Good. Rebecca had gone. I was all alone. Then I walked calmly to the center of the stage, looked up to the very back of the auditorium and said the last two lines of my audition speech without raising my voice in the slightest. It felt wonderful and now I had a whole script to myself too, so I could learn lots more. I hugged it close, then looked at the name on the top of the front page and felt my face turning pale. *Rebecca Carlisle.* She must have come back to look for her script so she could learn her lines tonight. Oh no! That meant I couldn't take it. That would be too cruel. But she'd left now, hadn't she? She wasn't likely to come back, so it would be pointless to leave the script in the wings. Rebecca would easily be able to borrow one from one of her friends, wouldn't she?

A few minutes later I was in the music department photocopying the whole script, because it wasn't fair to Rebecca to take her script, and I'd feel like the most selfish person in the world if she got chucked off the play for not learning her lines when it wasn't her fault. I wished the photocopier wasn't making so much noise though, because if anyone caught me doing this, I'd be in terrible trouble. Photocopiers are strictly off limits to all students. The teachers have to punch in a code to activate the machines, but I'd noticed that Mrs. Harrison, the music teacher, had one of the old-fashioned kinds of photocopier that didn't need a code. I must admit I was quite impressed with myself for thinking up this plan of mine. Now, all I had to do was give Rebecca her script back at dinner.

Oh no! Dinner!

I looked at my watch and nearly had a heart attack. It was six fifty-five. Dinner starts at six thirty and the sixth graders are supposed to be there by seven at the very latest. I was ridiculously late, and worse, Mia would be going absolutely frantic with worry about where I was. I just hoped like crazy that she hadn't told the duty staff I was missing or World War Three would break out. I hid the brand-new script behind the photocopier and set off to the cafeteria at my fastest gallop, clutching Rebecca's script.

I spotted her as soon as I went in and rushed over to her table. "I found this on the ground..."

Her eyes flew open and she grabbed it from me. "Oh thank you! You're my savior!" Then she frowned. "Where did you say you found it?"

"Just outside the main building."

"Someone must have picked your script up by mistake," said the girl next to Rebecca.

"Then dumped it when they realized their mistake," said Rebecca, wide-eyed. "Charming!"

I rolled my eyes, said "I know!" and went off to

get myself some sweet-and-sour chicken, feeling pleased that I seemed to have gotten away with an awful lot since school finished. But, unfortunately that wasn't quite true. As I sat down beside Mia she fixed me with a glare that was halfway between worried and accusing.

"Where have you been?"

"I...I've just..."

"What were you doing with that script? I saw you giving it to that girl."

"I..."

"I bet you went to a rehearsal, didn't you?"

And instantly all my friends' eyes were on me.

I was shocked and just said the first thing that came out of my mouth. "No I did not!"

"So why were you giving that girl a script?"

"I...found it on the ground outside."

"But...Georgie...I never know where you are these days, and even when you're right beside me I feel as though you're on another planet, sometimes." Mia's voice seemed to have shrunk and she looked really fed up, which instantly made me hate myself for being such a terrible best friend. I so wished I could admit that I'd been to the rehearsal, that I was reading *Little Women*, that I couldn't stop thinking about the play the whole time and that I really, really regretted being a stupid idiot and turning down a chance at a perfectly good part at the auditions. And finally, I'd give anything, *anything* in the world to make the clocks go back so I could change my ridiculous impulsive behavior.

But I couldn't turn the clocks back. And neither could I bring myself to admit everything to my friends. I was too ashamed.

Too ashamed by far.

Chapter Six

I sat at the back during quite a few rehearsals after that first one, without Miss Pritchard or anyone knowing I was there. I felt guilty about not telling Mia, but it would have been too awkward trying to explain why I wanted to keep going. I'd studied the script so much that I knew lots of it by heart, especially Amy's part, and sometimes it was hard to stay silent when I was desperate to prompt people who forgot a line, or hold in a sigh if anyone said a line badly.

It was during a rehearsal of a scene where Amy has lots to say, that I noticed Cara's voice sounding weak and scratchy.

It was obvious Miss Pritchard was anxious. "Is your throat hurting, Cara?"

Cara nodded. "Everyone's got coughs and colds and things at Beech House."

"Well, just say the lines quietly for today. The last thing we need is for you to lose your voice with the performances getting nearer."

So Cara did as she was told and people kept on missing their cues because they couldn't hear her properly. It was the most frustrating thing in the world, sitting there, knowing most of the lines and feeling certain I could have stood in and taken over the part. And of course, the moment that thought took root in my head I couldn't stop it growing and growing, feeding off my excitement. I started planning what to say to Miss Pritchard... *'Scuse me, Miss Pritchard, but I know all Cara's lines...*or maybe *'Scuse me, Miss Pritchard, I can easily take over if you want...* But what if she was furious at discovering I was attending a rehearsal when I wasn't in the play? It might be breaking the school rules. And even if it wasn't, I guessed she'd be unhappy that I hadn't asked permission to watch.

During the next few minutes Miss Pritchard had to stop the action three times to tell Cara to try and speak a teeny bit louder so the other actors could hear her, but it was obvious from the way Cara kept putting her hand on her throat that it was hurting her. It was on the fourth time that I simply couldn't restrain myself, and blurted out, "I'll do Cara's part if you want, Miss Pritchard – just to save her voice... I think I can..."

Miss Pritchard swung around and I saw her expression harden when she spotted me at the back. "How long have you been sitting up there? It's Georgie, isn't it?"

"Yes...I was just...watching."

"So I gather. You know, you're not supposed to watch rehearsals when you're not in the play."

"Sorry...yes, sorry, I mean, no...I didn't realize... only the thing is, I know some of the lines so I thought...I might be able to help, you see."

She nodded. "Right..." And for a wonderful moment I thought that was a signal for me to take over, so I jumped up, but she put her hand up like a traffic cop. "Whoa there!"

A few snickers broke out on the stage but I tried to ignore them.

Miss Pritchard spoke briskly. "Thank you for the offer, Georgie, but I'm afraid it's not *quite* as easy as all that."

I caught Cara smiling to herself as Miss Pritchard turned back to the stage, and there were more snickers, which made my temper rage because it was like she was sharing a joke with all the actors about the pathetic girl who thought she could step in and take over a main role, just like that. The final straw that made my blood boil was when Cara stared straight at me, tipped her head to the side and gave me a deliberately fake smile with mean eyes. She might as well have just come out and said, *You are such a loser.*

Miss Pritchard looked at her watch and it was as though I'd never spoken. "I think the best thing would be to skip this scene and move to the next one. Cara, go and see what your dorm mom says you need for your throat. Who is your dorm mom by the way?"

"Mrs. Bradley."

"Right. I'll have a word with her. Throat lozenges will do you good too. But most importantly, I want you to make a conscious effort to rest your voice at all times. Got that?"

Cara put on her most sugary expression and did a little croaky cough as she left the theater. Then Miss Pritchard clapped her hands and raised her voice, getting everyone organized as quickly as possible for the next scene, and I crept out of the back door, feeling the disappointment and the sadness start to mix in with my anger and weigh me down, like they had after my audition. There wasn't any point in anything anymore. I'd been so hoping that something might happen to give me a chance to be in the play after all. But now that chance was dead and buried.

I looked at my watch. Mia had probably gone down to Pets' Place to see her guinea pigs, Porgy and Bess. Katy might have gone with her to see Buddy, her rabbit. They often went at this time of day, after piano practice or clubs or whatever they'd been doing after school. I'm not all that into animals and I'm always joking with them about how nuts they are, wanting to keep stinky pets that need feeding and cleaning out all the time. But plodding off to find them right now, I didn't think they were nuts at all. In fact I even wished I had a pet myself. Just something to cuddle.

The door to the shed felt stiff, unless it was only me not having the knack of how to open it, but then it suddenly gave way and I kind of catapulted in and practically knocked Naomi over.

"Hey!"

"Oh sorry!"

"Georgie!" Mia was just putting one of her guinea pigs back in its hutch. She looked pretty amazed to see me.

"Hi...I...um...thought I'd find you here," I stammered.

"Wonders will never cease!" smiled Katy. Then she dumped Buddy in my arms. "Here. Hold him a minute."

"Do I have to?" I said, wrinkling my nose, because that's what they expected me to do. But really I loved the feel of the heavy bundle of fur.

"Look at Bess!" said Mia, coming over in a hurry to show me some new marking on her pet's fur. "It definitely wasn't this dark before."

"It's what happens in the winter," Katy said, sounding knowledgeable. Then she spoiled it. "Actually I don't know what I'm talking about."

Naomi laughed and so did I, but then I stopped abruptly because the memory of how fed up I was had started to seep back into this new little patch of happiness.

"Dinner time," said Naomi, looking at her watch. "Let's go. I'm starving."

Katy grabbed Buddy from me, buried her nose in his fur and said, "Night-night, my beautiful Buddy. Sleep tight, and if the bugs bite, bite 'em back!"

Then there was a flurry of petting and blowing kisses to every single animal in the place and the next moment we were out in the cold air, Katy and Naomi jogging on ahead and Mia and me walking behind. The closer we got to the cafeteria, the more I felt the big gloom taking me over. At least Mia hadn't asked me where I'd been or why I'd suddenly come along to Pets' Place – we'd just talked about winter and that had led to Christmas and what presents we were hoping to get. Maybe that explained my gloom, because there wasn't a single thing I wanted that could be wrapped up and put in a stocking.

I had the feeling something bad was going to happen from the moment we walked into the cafeteria and saw Cara talking to her friends. There were six of them all leaning forward in a tight little knot listening with big eyes as Cara held everyone's attention in her usual way. Part of me felt like marching over there and saying, "Huh! Call that saving your voice, Cara?" but the bigger part of me was afraid of what she might be telling them.

It was when I was having dessert that I found out. Two of Cara's friends threw me a quick glance as they walked past our table, then snickered really obviously.

"What's so funny?" Katy asked them indignantly.

"Nothing!" they told her. Then they went, but not before giving me another sneer.

Katy turned to me, looking horrified. "Why are they looking at you like that?"

My heart was beating faster but I shrugged and tried to sound as though I couldn't care less. "I dunno...Cara's probably made some joke about me not being in the play. I tell you, she's so immature..."

"*I'm* immature! Yeah right!"

I looked up and felt my face drain. Cara was standing there, hands on hips, giving me a nasty evil stare and I knew there was worse to come.

Her voice was croaky, and even disappeared altogether once, but it was still perfectly clear what she was saying. "Imagine thinking you can interrupt a rehearsal and ask to take over a main role when you're not even in the play." She leaned forward and practically spat at me. "And *why* aren't you in the play? I'll *tell* you why. Because you went into a pathetic little stress when you found out you weren't good enough for a main part, and refused to take the part of Susie Perkins, because you thought you were too good for a minor role. You think you're so special, Georgie Henderson, but you're *not*! Imagine asking to stand in for me. Like *that* would ever happen!"

Then she gave me a final glare and walked off. I had no idea what to do or say so I sat there completely rigid with a hurting throat, and waited to see what happened. And what happened was that Mia's arm went around me on one side and Naomi's on the other side, so then my throat hurt even more, but I used all my strength to stop myself from crying.

"She's horrible," said Mia.

"And she's a liar," said Katy, crossly.

"Yes—" Jess started to join in, but I interrupted her in a flat voice because I'd just kind of given in.

"She's not actually."

For once Katy sounded unsure of herself. "Wh... what?"

"I agree she's horrible," I went on in that same dead voice, "but actually..." I sighed. "...she's not a liar."

So then everyone was stuck for what to say.

It was Naomi who broke the uncomfortable silence. "Let's talk about it somewhere else."

"Yes, in the dorm after study hour," Mia finished off, patting my shoulder before she took her arm away. "We'll have a friendship meeting."

So that's what we did.

I somehow got through study hour, and then as

soon as it was over we sat on the rug in the middle of the dorm and I spilled everything out to them, all about how stupid I'd been to turn down the chance to play the role of Susie Perkins, how sad I was not to be involved with the play, and how pathetic I was to care so much. And they looked at me with big sympathetic eyes, which made me so grateful because I didn't deserve to have these sweet friends supporting me after the way I'd behaved.

"I know you won't believe me," I said in a small voice, "but I really *am* good at acting. I just had an awful audition because I tried to do it in the same way I'd always acted in elementary school, and it's obviously a much harder play. Also, Miss Pritchard said we had to bear in mind that the theater is bigger than the hall, and I thought she was trying to get us to really speak up, but now I think about it, I imagine she probably only said that for the people who are shy and naturally much quieter than me. It's embarrassing to think how loudly I must have yelled out those lines in the audition, actually! And now, I just can't stop thinking about the play the whole time."

"I knew you were still interested in it," said Katy, "because I saw *Little Women* on your desk."

"Yeah, me too," said Jess.

That gave me a little shock. I didn't think anyone had noticed. "Have you seen me reading the script as well?" I asked, feeling stupid.

"The script? You've got a copy of the script?" asked Mia.

I nodded. "I photocopied it from Rebecca's. Remember when you saw me give hers back to her?"

Katy frowned as though she was trying to figure out a difficult math problem. "So, you mean, you *have* been going to rehearsals?"

I felt my face getting hot as I nodded. "Mmm."

"Didn't Miss Pritchard mind?" was all Mia said.

"She didn't realize I was there...until today."

There was another silence and I guessed this was the moment when they were all remembering those words of Cara's... *Imagine asking to stand in for me. Like* that *would ever happen!* It was so embarrassing I felt like getting under my blanket, curling into a tight ball and refusing to come out.

But just as I was bracing myself for someone to bring up the horrible subject, Jess's cell ringtone broke the silence, and made me jump.

"Oh, that's my phone telling me it's time for *The Fast Lane*! I set my reminder."

A feeling of relief swept through me. This was everyone's favorite TV program and they'd all go racing off any second now. Good, I didn't have to talk about what had happened in the rehearsal.

Jess was first to get up. "Are you coming, Georgie?" she asked hesitantly.

I shook my head. Even the thought of *The Fast Lane* did nothing to cheer me up.

"Will you be okay?" asked Naomi, getting up with Katy.

"I'm staying here," said Mia firmly.

So the others went and even though I tried to persuade Mia to go, she wouldn't. "I still want to talk to you, Georgie."

The moment we were alone she asked me the question I was dreading answering, but because there was only Mia there now, I didn't feel like getting under the blanket anymore.

"What exactly did Cara mean about...offering to stand in for her?"

I heaved a huge sigh and looked down when I spoke. "Cara couldn't do the part right today because of her throat. No one could hear what she was saying, and I've learned almost all of Amy's lines, so I...offered to say them to...you know...to help Miss Pritchard out."

"And...what did Miss Pritchard say?"

I sighed again. "She looked at me like I was a little

kid and said it wasn't as easy as all that. And Cara looked at me like I was a total loser."

"That is *so* unfair."

"It made me mad…because *they* don't know what I can and can't do."

"And anyway you were only trying to help. Miss Pritchard should have been grateful. She should at least have let you try it."

Mia was being such a good friend, and that made me feel horribly guilty. "Do you hate me for going to all those rehearsals and not telling you, Mia?"

She bit her lip. "I knew that was where you were."

"What, you mean you saw me go in or something?"

She shook her head. "No, I just knew. I think Katy and Naomi guessed too. We were all just kind of waiting for you to say something." Mia smiled. "It's obvious if you think about it. I mean, ever since the auditions you've been inside your own little world, you haven't even watched *The Fast Lane* for three weeks, you're reading *Little Women* and you're talking in your sleep."

"Talking in my sleep? Oh no! What have I been saying?"

"I can't remember because it didn't make sense,

but you seemed to be having a conversation with two people named Meg and Jo!"

She smiled, then we both giggled. "Sort of a giveaway, then!" I admitted.

Mia suddenly jumped up and pulled me to my feet, looking excited. "Hey, Georgie, will you say some of Amy's lines for me?"

"What here? Now?"

She nodded.

"I can't. I'm too fed up about everything."

I knew I'd kind of spoiled our conversation, because Mia looked so disappointed, but there was nothing I could do about it. My emotions had been shaken up. If I'd tried to say the lines at that moment in time, they wouldn't have come out right at all. And that night, after everyone had gone to sleep, I lay there feeling completely fed up, and in the end I got out of bed, found a pencil and went and altered the sign on the door to our dorm. I didn't think anyone else would notice, and I didn't much care whether they did or they didn't. I just wanted to punish myself. It wasn't right that it said Georgie the Actress. Standing in the silent corridor I stared at the new word I'd written beside my name.

Georgie the Loser.

Yes, that was the truth.

*   *   *

The following day it was Saturday morning school. It always seems unfair that we have to have classes on Saturday mornings as well as during the rest of the week, but at least we're free after that and there are often really good trips and things organized for the rest of the weekend. I was having a horrible time in French because I seemed to be the only person in the class who couldn't tell the time in French (unless it was something o'clock), when in came Miss Pritchard and asked Mam'zelle Clemence if she could have a word with Georgie Henderson.

Everyone was suddenly completely still and I knew they'd be tuning in to what Miss Pritchard was saying to me. She came over and her loud whisper seemed to go pinging off all four walls.

"Cara's lost her voice completely now, Georgie, and I had an idea. I was wondering, as you want so much to be involved in the play..."

My heart leaped and I sat up straighter. *Yes?*

"...if you'd like to stand in for Alice Dunbar, who's got the part of Hannah, the housekeeper. Alice is willing to read Cara's lines. Just until Cara is better."

I swallowed and felt a rush of disappointment, but it quickly dissolved as I realized at least I'd still be involved in the play. I guessed that Miss Pritchard had chosen Alice Dunbar because she's the brainiest girl in the world and she'd be able to say the lines without hesitation, and wouldn't bury her head in the script because she'd be able to read ahead and remember enough words to look up for quite a while without losing her place. Yes, Alice was definitely a great choice except – and this is a big *except* – that I'd watched her acting the part of Hannah and I didn't think she was a very good actress. She still sounded like Alice Dunbar, no matter what words were coming out of her mouth.

All this whizzed through my mind in a microsecond and I so wanted to tell Miss Pritchard that it would be much easier if she just let me do Cara's part, as then she wouldn't need to take Alice out of her own role. But I stopped myself because, after all, I wasn't going to be acting in the real play, I was just helping out until Cara's voice came back. So I simply said, "Yes, that's fine," in my most mature voice, which earned me a smile as Miss Pritchard dropped a crisp script on my desk.

"I've highlighted your lines. We're starting immediately after lunch. See you later."

Then she was gone. Just like that.

"So let us continue with telling the time," said

Mam'zelle Clemence, trying to get the class back on course. She looked directly at me. "Georgie, *quelle heure est-il?*"

I looked at the clock. It was exactly half past ten. "*Dix heures et demie,*" I said without hesitation.

"*Oui!*" said Mam'zelle Clemence. "*Très bien!*"

And I smiled with happiness, not because I'd gotten the time right, but because I suddenly realized I'd actually gotten myself a part in the play after all, even if it was only for a while. And my day that had seemed so dull and dark was now filled with little dancing lights.

Chapter Seven

The role of Hannah consisted of quite a few appearances but only about ten lines and I had a pretty good idea of nearly half of them by the end of French. I can't say Mam'zelle Clemence had been over the moon when she'd noticed the script on my lap. In fact she'd given me another lecture about my lack of concentration and warned me about my report card, but I was too excited about the play for anything like a little telling-off to worry me.

Cara wasn't at lunch, thank goodness, and I know it was horrible of me but I hoped her voice would take ages to come back so I'd get the best possible chance to impress Miss Pritchard, just in case someone had to drop out at the last minute, and then I'd be first choice to step in and take the part. I bolted down my tuna sandwich then raced over to the theater, only to find I was first to arrive. When Miss Pritchard came into the auditorium a few minutes later to find me learning my lines, she blinked in big surprise.

"That's what I like to see!" Then she started explaining the storyline and showed me where I'd be standing on the stage for the first section we were going to rehearse.

"Yes, I know," I said.

She paused mid-sentence but then went on as though I hadn't spoken. "And Jo will appear from just over here…"

"Yes, I know."

"What do you mean, you *know*?" She sounded a little exasperated.

"I've seen you rehearsing this part."

As soon as I'd spoken I wished I could shove the words straight back in my great big mouth. Now I'd given it away that I'd sat in on more than one rehearsal. The look on Miss Pritchard's face said she didn't like what she was hearing but she was prepared to let it go. "And I know you're only reading the lines but it'll help the others if you try to speak in character," she continued, "so keep in mind that your character is slower and older than anyone else in the household. Only…" Miss Pritchard looked as though she'd just remembered something. "…don't overdo it."

I wished she hadn't said those last three words because she was obviously thinking back to when I'd done my terrible audition and I'd really been hoping she might have forgotten about that. It was tempting to quickly remind her that I'd not realized the theater was amplified and everything, but the new sensible mature Georgie just nodded and kept quiet.

It was while Miss Pritchard was explaining to me about another scene that everyone started drifting into the theater. She was pointing to a particular speech of Amy's on the script. "Don't wait for Alice to finish what she's saying, Georgie. You need to interrupt her about here…"

"Yes, I know."

Now she really was exasperated. "Georgie, are you sure you're actually taking in what I'm saying?"

"Yes, every word," I assured her, nodding my head vigorously. Then I quickly changed it to a simple "Yes," in case she thought I was being smart.

"Okay." She nodded then strode off the stage and told everyone to get into their places for Act One, Scene Three.

"What are *you* doing here?" one of the eighth graders asked me, which made me feel like the lowest form of pond life.

"Standing in for Alice Dunbar," I said, desperately trying to find my place on the script.

"Alice is *here,* though."

"Yes, but Cara's sick so Alice is reading her part and I'm—"

"Georgie, one thing you'll have to learn is that there isn't time to talk during rehearsals," came Miss Pritchard's no-nonsense voice.

"But—"

"Top left wing, Georgie!" she interrupted, pointing to where I had to go.

"Yes, I know."

Whoops. Now she looked completely stressed out, and we'd not even started.

My first speech was the longest and also the one that I knew best. Hannah the housekeeper was supposed to be giving Jo a little talking-to, not exactly telling her off, but speaking sternly to make the point that Jo hadn't been pulling her weight. All I had to do was make my entrance at the right moment, remember the words and say them slowly with an old voice, but not *too* slowly and not *too* old. I felt myself tensing up as the cue got closer and I rolled my shoulders and neck around to make myself relax. A couple of the eighth graders exchanged a look when I did that but I tried to ignore them and walked on with my script by my side and my eyes on Camilla Tomkinson, who was playing the part of Jo.

It was weird but as I spoke the lines to her I saw how the expression in her eyes changed from mild surprise to a kind of frustration and embarrassment, and I felt as though I really was talking to Jo, because it was exactly how I knew Jo would have reacted, and that spurred me on to do my own part even better. I almost got through the whole speech without a slip, but could have kicked myself when I forgot the last few words and had to look at the script.

"Well done!" said Miss Pritchard, but I didn't know if she was talking to me or to Camilla.

"Was my voice too slow?" I whispered to Camilla, when I'd finished my part of the scene and we were both in the wings together.

"No, it was good," was all she said before she had to go back onstage for her next appearance. I sneaked around the side to slip back into the auditorium, which is what you're supposed to do when you're not needed for a while.

Miss Pritchard was concentrating on the action on the stage when I sat down with all the other waiting people, so she didn't say anything to me. In fact, I don't even think she noticed me. I just had to hope that she thought I'd done okay. Then I went back to learning the lines for my next scene, even though I knew I wouldn't be on for ages. At least Camilla had said I was good, and that made me feel great. I went into a little daydream, going back over our scene together and remembering that look in her eyes. It was funny how my own acting had improved just because of the way Camilla had acted. I think professional actors call it "feeding off" each other. I mean, if you're trying to make your role as realistic as possible but the person opposite you sounds wooden, you've got a much tougher job on your hands. That's what it was like in elementary school. But it was different here. There were lots of great actresses here.

My eyes were glued to the stage when Alice Dunbar made her entrance. I noticed her knuckles were white from holding the script so tightly but she said Amy's lines completely fluently and without a single mistake, exactly as I'd imagined she would. It was Camilla who had to say the next lines and she was supposed to be very upbeat and a little bit wild, but she didn't do it quite as well as usual and Miss Pritchard had to remind her about clasping her hands together on certain words. Camilla nodded and pursed her lips, then did the speech again. It was a little better, but not much, and I could tell from the look on Camilla's face that she wasn't happy with her performance.

For the next hour Alice was onstage more than she was off, and had lots and lots to say. I don't think she made a single slip because she was mainly reading, but it sounded so completely different from the way Cara does the role that I didn't get the same feeling of being in the middle of the world of the four sisters. I don't think Miss Pritchard did either because she kept on stopping the action and making people try things again.

It was when Alice was doing a scene with Savannah Shaw, who is playing Beth, that Miss Pritchard started correcting the way Alice was saying her lines. "Try and commit those last two sentences to memory, then say them as though you're an exuberant eleven-year-old with not a care in the world, Alice. Maybe you could make your voice a touch harsher – not so smooth. Can you try that?"

Alice did as she was told and it instantly sounded much better.

"Nice!" said Miss Pritchard. "Stick to that way of talking, all right?"

But it didn't work. In no time at all the reading voice was back and Miss Pritchard had to repeat what she'd just said. "I know it's hard when you're only reading from the script, Alice, but as you get to know the part, and you don't have to worry about following the words all the time, I'm sure you'll be able to relax into acting the role soon."

Immediately big alarm bells started to ring. The way Miss Pritchard was talking made it sound like Alice was taking over the role. And I wasn't the only one to wonder what was going on. Camilla was suddenly talking urgently to Miss Pritchard, with Savannah not far behind.

"But Alice is only standing in for Cara while she's lost her voice, isn't she?"

"Cara should be back soon, shouldn't she?"

There was a pause, and I made my hands into fists and pressed my thumbs against my mouth waiting for what Miss Pritchard would say, and stopping anything I might regret later from escaping from my mouth.

"I'm sure Cara will be fine soon, but as a precaution I've suggested to Alice that she tries to learn Amy's part so she can understudy if necessary." Miss Pritchard smiled around at everyone and you could tell she was trying to convince people that her idea was a good one, even though it was obvious from all the glum faces that no one was very impressed. "We're very lucky that Alice is such a quick learner, is all I can say!"

I pressed my thumbs against my lips even harder, because I was bursting to tell Miss Pritchard that if she wanted an exuberant eleven-year-old, there was one sitting over here who already knew just about all the lines.

"Georgie..." Her eyes clamped onto me. "You seem to have learned quite a bit of the role of Hannah already, which is great, and I'd like you to act as understudy for Alice." An extra note of firmness came into her voice. "It's tough being an understudy because of course it's very likely that you won't actually get to be in the play, so it takes a very special person to be prepared for the hard work of learning all the lines when you might not get a chance to perform them. You've obviously got much less to learn than Alice does, Georgie, but still it's good of you to take on the responsibility." She clapped her hands together, then turned it into a kind of satisfied rub, as if to say, *Good, now that we all know where we are, let's move on.*

At the end of the rehearsal I went out just behind Camilla and Savannah and I could hear what they were saying even though they were only speaking quietly.

"It's no good with Alice doing Cara's part, is it?"

"I know. And she doesn't even like doing it. She told me. I feel really sorry for her actually."

"Trouble is..." Camilla was speaking so softly I could only just hear her. "...I don't think she'll be able to say the lines right, even when she's learned them."

Savannah nodded and I could see her face as she turned to Camilla, looking as though she was apologizing about something. I knew they didn't like saying mean things about Alice. They were nice girls. "She still sounds like Hannah the housekeeper, doesn't she?"

There was a pause, then Camilla's voice went a little louder. "Yes, but Georgie's good, isn't she?"

"I know! I was kind of surprised."

"Me too. Should we go to Beech House and see how Cara is?"

"Yeah, come on."

I broke into a run after they'd gone because I suddenly felt like telling Mia all about the conversation I'd just heard and how I'd done at the rehearsal. I knew she'd be proud of me. So would Grace, the wonder sportswoman, if she could see the speed I was covering the ground right now! It was only because I wanted to get back to perfecting my lines once I'd seen Mia. Inside Hazeldean I flew up to the practice rooms. Mia wasn't there, so I tried the dorm and came across Grace getting changed.

"Georgie, you've been running!" She was grinning at me but then she suddenly turned deadly serious. "Is everything okay? You look terrible."

"Well thanks for that!" I said. "Everything's fine and I haven't had a heart attack yet so you can relax."

"Oh sorry, Georgie!" she giggled. "It's just that I'm not used to seeing you all out of breath." She pointed to my desk where there was a big note propped up. "Mia left that for you about five minutes ago."

"Oh, she's in the art wing with Jess and Katy and Naomi," I said, reading the note quickly. "They're all painting the backdrop for the second act."

Grace nodded. "I know. Jess tried to get me to do it too, but I've just been in the gym and now I've got a volleyball match."

"See you later then, Grace. Good luck!"

At first I thought I might go and help with the painting, but I guessed they'd be packing up since it was practically time for dinner, so I decided to go back to the theater and feel the magic of that wonderful big stage again. I was just outside the front entrance when Mia came rushing up.

"Hey Georgie! We've been painting one of the sets for the play. Did you get my note?" She didn't let me reply, just went on gabbling. "It's supposed to be the living room wall with the window in the middle, and the art teacher's done the view through the window of next-door's yard. You're going to love it. It's stunning!" She suddenly clasped my hands. "Oh sorry, I should have asked, was it good being Hannah? How did it go?"

"Great! In fact it was so good that I was just going back to have another try on the stage!"

We both laughed and Mia said she wanted to come and hear me saying some of Hannah's lines and I realized guiltily that I hadn't heard her playing piano for ages. "After study hour can I hear your pieces, Mia?"

She nodded happily. "You can tell me if they've improved since the last time you heard them, okay?"

On the way to the theater I told her what I'd heard Savannah and Camilla saying after the rehearsal. Mia listened with a serious look on her face and then said, "Maybe Cara'll be better soon. My mom lost her voice over fall break but it only lasted a few days. Then it was good as new again."

I hoped Mia was right, and as we went into the theater I got a sudden shock because I'd just realized something weird. Here I was, actually wishing for Cara to get better when a) I couldn't stand the girl and b) if she did get better it would mean that I absolutely definitely wouldn't be in the play, not even in a small role. I sighed and realized something even more shocking. I'd finally accepted that, much as I was desperate to have the part of Amy, *that* was never going to happen when it was only two weeks until the performances, so the next best thing would be for Cara's voice to come back, as she's about ten times better at acting the part than poor Alice, and I cared about the play. I wanted it to be good.

"Okay, I'll sit in the audience and you pretend to be Hannah!" said Mia, rushing up to the fifth row and sitting right in the middle with an expectant look on her face.

"Oh, can't I pretend to be Amy?"

Mia giggled. "You can pretend to be Prince Harry if you want! I don't care. I'm just happy to sit here like the Queen and have my own private performance!"

So then we were both giggling because Mia doesn't often crack jokes, which made it even funnier.

"Only you'd better hurry up," Mia went on, looking suddenly serious, "or we'll be late for dinner."

I did one of Amy's sad speeches from near the end of the play when she's just heard how sick Beth is, and when I'd finished Mia didn't say anything, which was a little worrying, except that when I looked carefully at her I realized she was almost in tears.

"You really *are* a good actress, Georgie. That was… amazing!"

"Oh thanks, Mia!" I said, breaking into a little tap routine of happiness. Then I rushed up to the auditorium and pulled her to her feet. "Come on – dinner! I could eat an ox!"

Chapter Eight

At the beginning of the next rehearsal everyone was asking how Cara was, and I was full of envy. I'd love it if people were desperate for me to come back after an illness because I was such a stunning actress.

"I've got good news and bad news," announced Miss Pritchard, trying to sound all light-hearted, though it was obvious from her eyes that she didn't feel like that really. "The bad news is that poor Cara's got laryngitis and won't be able to be in the play…" I couldn't help joining in with the gasp of disbelief mixed with disappointment that went up. "But the good news…" Miss Pritchard gave Alice a big smile "…is that Alice has learned all of Amy's lines!" The smile came swiveling around to me. "And how are you doing with Hannah's lines, Georgie?"

I nodded a little bleakly. "Yes, I've learned them all."

No one said a word and I actually felt sorry for Alice now because she looked so miserable. I only hoped she was going to act better than last time, then maybe we'd get some of the old atmosphere back. As I went to take my place in the wings I thought, *Oh well, at least I can tell Mom and Grandma that I have actually got a part now, even if it's not exactly the biggest one in the world.*

It was true that Alice had learned every single word and she was saying them with much more expression than the last time, but still there was something not quite right, and everyone was obviously feeling it, because the play seemed so dull.

"Well I can only hope that you're all saving yourselves for the performances," said Miss Pritchard, looking grave. "Quite frankly this play is as flat as a pancake, and if I were sitting in the audience I would have seriously thought of going home by now." A silence fell over all the actors. "I don't know what's the matter with you all."

At the end of the rehearsal everyone trooped out and Miss Pritchard sat down alone at her desk. I was the last to leave the theater and I watched her staring into space tapping her pencil on her lips before I let the door close behind me. Then I stood still and felt my heart starting to bang against my ribs. If Miss Pritchard would just give me the chance to show her how I could play the part of Amy, I absolutely knew I could cheer her up. In fact I could cheer everyone up, because I'd definitely do it better than Alice. I pushed the door open and she looked up and frowned at me. "What do you want, Georgie?"

Her frown deepened and all my excitement and courage dissolved. I *mustn't* be impulsive. It only got me into trouble.

"I left my...oh, it's all right. I thought I'd left something, but..."

She suddenly fixed her eyes on me intently. "Georgie?"

"Yes?"

Then she sighed. "Shut the door as you go out, all right."

So I left her tapping her lip with her pencil again, and crept sadly away.

*   *   *

"Is Cara still sick?" someone asked at the start of the next rehearsal.

"Yes," said Miss Pritchard in a bit of a snap. "I've told you Cara won't be able to be in the play. Where's Georgie Henderson?"

I stiffened.

Then she spotted me. "Come here a moment, Georgie." Quite a few others came closer to hear what she was going to say but she shooed them away. "Off you go. I want a word with Georgie."

Everyone scuttled away. Miss Pritchard narrowed her eyes as though she was a detective and had almost solved a murder but was just trying to find that last piece of the puzzle.

"I saw you on the stage in the theater the other day," she began, looking very serious.

My heart hammered as I remembered Mia watching me from the fifth row. "Sorry, Miss Pritchard. I didn't realize I wasn't allowed—"

She shook her head and flapped her hand impatiently. "No...I... The point is I heard you saying some of Amy's lines..."

I gulped and waited.

"How much of the part have you actually learned?"

"All of it."

She took a step backward. "*All* of it. Are you sure?"

Now I knew what people meant when they talked about walking on eggshells. Something told me I must be very, very careful. If only I had Naomi whispering the right answers into my ear. But actually I was in a state of shock now, and speaking was out of the question, so I just made a noise instead.

Miss Pritchard's eyes were like slits. "Is that a yes?"

"Mmmhmm."

"So you're telling me you've learned all of Amy's lines?"

"Mmmhmm."

"I'd like to hear you saying a few more. Is that all right?" She wasn't exactly smiling at me, but she was definitely giving me an encouraging look. All the same, I couldn't make any words come out.

"Mmm."

"Are you all right, Georgie? Please don't tell me you've lost your voice too?"

"No." I cleared my throat. "I'm okay…"

"Good. Choose any speech you want and go onto the stage."

"What about…?" I was looking around for Alice.

It felt a little embarrassing suddenly launching into one of her speeches right in front of her.

"I've talked with Alice. She knows you're having a try." Miss Pritchard clapped her hands. "Okay, girls, can we have a little quiet? I've asked Georgie to try one of Amy's speeches."

And the next minute I was in the middle of the stage wishing I could just have a cue from someone and then I'd feel more natural about acting with everyone staring at me and probably wondering what on earth was going on.

"I'll do the part when Beth is dying and Amy's at her bedside." I glanced at Savannah, who was playing the part of Beth, to see if she might offer to lie down and pretend to be sick like she did in that scene, but she just stood there looking as puzzled as everyone else.

"Savannah, go and lie on the couch, please," said Miss Pritchard. So Savannah did as she was told, and closed her eyes and I realized immediately that I'd made a big mistake choosing this part because it was the most emotional part of the play and although I could make tears come when I practiced alone, I was far too nervous for that to happen right now. In fact I wasn't sure that I could do the speech at all. But everyone was waiting. I had to do it.

I stared at Savannah's still face and tried with all my imagination to turn it into Beth's face, but it wasn't working, so then I tried to imagine it was Mia. Mia dying? That would be unbearable. I clung to that awful thought and began the speech. After only a few seconds there were tears in my eyes, blurring my vision and making my voice shaky. Then Savannah suddenly opened her own eyes and I saw that she was almost crying too, and in that split second I stopped thinking about Mia and all I could see was Beth, overcome with emotion because she knew she was seeing her sister for the last time. I leaned over and put my face next to hers for a second like it said in the script, and Savannah said her line in a really thin sad voice, just as Beth would have and then a few of my tears brimmed over and landed on her sweatshirt, and a moment later I had to stop because everyone was clapping and whooping like crazy.

Savannah shot up and gave me a big bear hug. "That was so cool, Georgie. You made me act out of my skin!"

And when I looked at Miss Pritchard I saw that she was actually wiping the corner of her eye with her finger, and her face didn't look at all in control like it normally does. Then Alice came leaping over to me and I got another hug. "Thank you! Thank you! Thank you! I hated trying to be Amy. I'll be able to go back to Hannah now!" And everyone laughed and started hugging Alice.

The clapping was the best sound in the world until Miss Pritchard spoke, and then *that* was the best sound in the world. "Well, folks, I think we've got a new Amy!"

Major tingles were breaking out all over me but I just needed to double-check something. "So I'm not the understudy. I really am going to actually act Amy in the play?"

Miss Pritchard spoke quietly but her eyes were dancing. "You certainly are!"

"Yesssss!" I punched the air about ten times and jumped up and down and felt like doing handsprings all the way across the stage, except that if I tried even a single one I'd collapse and probably break a leg. And then I laughed my head off because it suddenly seemed amazingly funny to think of the words "break a leg," as that's what people always say to actors to wish them luck on the first night.

"Okay, let's get down to business!" said Miss Pritchard.

And the next hour was total magic.

* * *

For three days I didn't come down off cloud nine. Mia and I kept high-fiving each other and screeching "Georgie is Amy!" at the tops of our voices. Miss Carol and Miss Fosbrook both hugged me and said they were delighted. Miss Jennings told me that when she'd first heard I was going to audition she didn't think I had a ghost of a chance, but she was really pleased I'd managed to pull it off. I e-mailed Mom with the fantastic news about getting a part and she called me and said it was absolutely wonderful and she was dying to see the performance, and all my friends agreed that it was the most exciting thing ever. I just felt one little tug of sadness that Dad wouldn't be able to see me because of his business trip. If only we'd known how everything was going to turn out.

"Just think, only five days till the first performance!" said Jess. "And then three wonderful weeks of Christmas vacation!"

Another little dark cloud drifted across my sunny skies at the thought of the holidays, because of course holidays meant report cards. I'd really tried hard to concentrate in classes but it didn't seem to have done much good, so I knew I'd be in for a rocket when I got home, especially as Dad wouldn't have even seen me acting, which might have softened the blow of the bad grades a little. But I shook that annoying black cloud out of my glowing picture and tuned into all the arrangements that my friends were making to see each other. Grace was the only one who wouldn't get to see any of the rest of us over the break because she was going back to Thailand to be with her family. She said she'd try to arrange for Jess to stay with her over the next break at Easter though, which made Jess very excited. And I was going to Mia's for a few days near the end of the break, which I was looking forward to like crazy.

Having my costume fitting was great fun. The dress that Cara had been going to wear was a little tight, so another one had been made quickly and Katy had designed and helped to make it, and it fit me perfectly! I never ever thought I'd enjoy wearing a mauve dress that went in at the waist and then flared out down to the ground, and had a little lace collar and puffed sleeves, but I absolutely loved it. Admiring myself in the mirror, I reminded myself of my little sister, who loves dressing up as much as I used to. The dress got me totally into the character of Amy and made me feel as though I was living in the nineteenth century. In fact, putting my school uniform back on afterward felt a bit depressing.

Another exciting moment was the first time we had a rehearsal with the four singing narrators and the band, which consisted of Mrs. Harrison on piano and five other girls playing string and wind instruments. The narrators simply walked on at the end of various scenes, and sang songs which linked up the events of the play, because if we'd been acting every single thing that happened in *Little Women* the play would go on forever. Sometimes the narrators sang solos and sometimes duets and sometimes all four of them sang together. Their voices were absolutely beautiful and they made the play even more moving than it already was. In fact I simply had to give a demonstration to my friends one evening after study hour. They sat on Grace's bed while I stood on the rug and belted out the tunes, but I couldn't remember half the words so I just sang "la la la" at the top of my voice.

Miss Carol came in right in the middle to tell us to get ready for bed, and after the others had gone off to the bathroom she looked as though she was about to say something to me. In fact she actually opened her mouth to speak, but then seemed to change her mind, and patted me on the back instead. I thought she was going to bustle me along because I was taking ages to get my washbag, but instead she just gave me this really funny smile, kind of pitying.

I didn't think anything of it at the time, but later when I was lying in bed, I couldn't stop thinking about it. I told myself it was probably nothing, but all the same it took me ages to get to sleep that night.

Chapter Nine

The following day Miss Pritchard came to look for me as I was finishing my lunch. There was something about the serious look on her face that made me shiver with nervousness. She said she wanted to talk to me and my mind flashed straight back to that smile Miss Carol had given me. She'd felt sorry for me at that moment and now I was positive I knew why. I could just feel it in my bones. We went to the vice-principal's office because Miss Pritchard thought that would be quieter than the cafeteria. She wasn't smiling but she definitely wasn't angry. My mouth felt completely dry and my chest was tight. Before she uttered a single word I knew what she was going to say.

"Georgie, we've got a difficult situation, I'm afraid."

"Cara's better, isn't she?" I blurted out.

"Yes, she is. She's recovered much faster than her dorm mom thought she would. And I've had to make a decision about what to do." She was speaking quickly as though she suddenly wanted to get it over with. I held my breath. "I think the best and fairest plan is for the two of you to share the role of Amy."

I nodded slowly, letting out my breath and feeling a massive relief that I wasn't going to lose the role of Amy after all. Then I started trying to work out whether Cara and I would actually have to talk to each other.

"Cara's parents have been contacted and fortunately they're very happy to attend the Friday evening performance and take Cara back home for the holidays immediately after the show. That's what lots of parents of students who aren't in the play are doing. And we don't need to contact your parents because I understand they're coming on Saturday."

"It's just Mom," I said bleakly. "Dad can't come."

"But you've got your grandmother, and is it your little sister…?"

I nodded. "Roxanne."

"I'm sure she'll enjoy it. How old is she?"

"Six." I smiled to myself at the thought of Roxanne watching *Castles in the Air*. She wouldn't understand most of it, but I knew she'd still love it. Then my brain started fast-forwarding. "What's going to happen at…"

Miss Pritchard must have been reading my mind. "I think Cara needs to play Amy at the next rehearsal because it's been a while since she's done it. I'm sure you agree that makes sense?"

I nodded and pictured myself sitting in the front row. I wasn't looking forward to it one little bit, especially as Cara probably hated me more than ever, now I'd done the very thing she'd said would never ever happen – I'd taken over *her* role.

I was thinking about Mia as I went into the theater after school, because this was the day she was doing her piano exam. I'd already wished her good luck about a million times but earlier we'd frantically wished each *other* good luck. I looked at my watch and realized that she might even be playing her scales at that very moment so I closed my eyes and sent her my best vibes, then sat down in the front row, which felt weird. My heart started beating faster when I heard Cara's voice, but I deliberately didn't look over toward the stage where I knew she'd be standing in the center of a big group of people.

"The doctor said it was amazing how quickly I recovered. Apparently laryngitis can affect your voice for weeks."

Miss Pritchard raised her hands for silence and quickly told everyone that it was great to have Cara back. "Cara and Georgie are sharing the role of Amy now, with Cara doing the Friday night performance and Georgie, the Saturday," she explained in her bright voice. I glanced over at Cara but she wasn't looking at me. She had her eyes on some distant spot in the auditorium. "Cara will take the part in the technical rehearsal on Thursday, when we'll have all the lights and amplification, and Georgie will take the part for the dress rehearsal on Friday afternoon." She paused and looked around. "The thing I want everyone to remember is that no two actors ever interpret a role in quite the same way, and the same is true of Cara and Georgie. They're both giving their own individual interpretation, and both of them are wonderful." She paused again as if to let those words of hers sink in, then she suddenly turned brisk. "Okay, let's get started."

It felt weird sitting alone in the front row watching everyone acting after I'd been so involved only the day before. All the actors had to stay backstage for the whole rehearsal because Miss Pritchard wanted the play to be precisely how it would be in the actual performances. Cara stumbled a few times, which wasn't any wonder when she'd not done it for ages, but I saw Savannah and Camilla rolling their eyes at one another when they probably thought no one was looking. They didn't seem to be putting as much as usual into their performances, and twice Miss Pritchard told them firmly to try to keep up their energy. Rebecca was fine all through the first act, but then Cara seemed to be really struggling to act like she used to in the second act, and that somehow affected Rebecca because she kept on forgetting her lines and seemed really nervous. So Miss Pritchard had to have a talk with three of the four main people.

"I know you're ready for the Christmas vacation," she said in her I'm-trying-to-be-patient voice, "and you've worked incredibly hard to achieve all you've achieved with this play, but we're almost there now so try to remember it's a showcase for the school and I'm not accepting anything less than your best performances on Friday and Saturday. Rebecca, there's no need to be nervous. Just relax, because you're absolutely fine. Maybe have a quick look over your lines tonight."

Camilla suddenly came forward and said, "Yes but—" then stopped abruptly, as if she'd changed her mind.

"But what?" asked Miss Pritchard, not unkindly.

"It's okay."

I saw Cara sucking her lips in, and noticed how pale her face was at that moment. Quite a few people exchanged looks though nobody spoke, but I wasn't sure what that was all about. Then Miss Pritchard told everyone to get a good night's sleep and people started drifting out quietly.

I went straight to find Mia because I was dying to find out how she'd done. She'd been so nervous all through the day and I was really hoping she'd managed to shake it off for her actual exam.

It was when I was only about ten yards away from Hazeldean that someone called out my name and I turned around to see Cara, which gave me a big shock I can tell you. I organized my face so it was set in my hardest expression, because she was bound to say something nasty. Then I waited for her to catch up to me, because no way was I going to take a single step toward her. But as she got closer I realized she looked pale.

"I wanted to ask you something," she said quietly.

It was confusing me that she wasn't being mean. I didn't know how to react. "Wh...what?"

A part of me wondered whether this was all a very smart trick, and any minute now her friends might jump out from behind a tree and start sneering and saying cruel things about how I thought I'd gotten the part of Amy but now that wasn't quite true after all.

She looked down, then back up again. "I was wondering...whether...you'd like to act in both performances?"

I couldn't speak I was so shocked. The great Cara Ravenscroft was actually offering me the chance to have the role of Amy all to myself. No. It had to be a joke. I stared at her, waiting for her mask to drop.

"Yeah right."

"No, I mean it." Her face looked paler than ever and her eyes were full of big worry. If this was an act then she was the best actress I'd ever come across.

I tried to sound businesslike. "Has your laryngitis come back?"

She shook her head. "It's just that...the others don't seem to be...acting so well now..." She looked as though she was going to cry and I suddenly knew for certain that this wasn't an act.

"I think it's like Miss Pritchard said...everyone's really tired..." I said carefully.

"No, it's not that. I saw Camilla and Savannah exchange a look and I was sure it was because they thought I wasn't as good as I used to be, and that made me even worse, and then I heard Camilla whispering to Savannah when we were all leaving the theater. She was trying to persuade Savannah to say something to Miss Pritchard."

"Well that doesn't prove anything." I didn't really believe what I was saying, but Cara was in a terrible state and I felt genuinely sorry for her.

"The thing is, Georgie, Savannah *did* go and talk to Miss Pritchard but I couldn't hear what she said because she had her back to me and she was talking really quietly, but I heard Miss Pritchard's reply..."

I bit my lip.

"She said, 'No, I'm sorry, Savannah, that would be completely unfair. You were perfectly happy with Cara before she was sick, so you just need to be professional about this and adapt to whichever one of them is playing the role.'" Cara's eyes filled with tears. "So you see, they really prefer it when you're playing Amy, and I don't want the play to be ruined or everyone'll say it's my fault."

My head was bursting with swirling lights. Savannah and Camilla preferred my acting to Cara's. Cara herself wanted me to take over the role completely. I'd totally proved myself now. I could actually play Amy on my own merits and not just as an understudy because of Cara being sick. All my friends and my family would be so proud of me. I could just picture their faces, especially my gran's. She'd probably be the proudest of all. But...the swirling lights slowed down and stopped as I looked at Cara's crumpled face. The problem was, I wouldn't be proud of my*self*. In fact I'd be disappointed in myself.

And in that moment I made a decision.

I put my arm around Cara and concentrated hard on the white lie I was about to tell. "Camilla and Savannah weren't happy when I first took over from you, you know, but then they...got used to me. And they just have to get used to you again. I bet you anything they'll be fine in the technical rehearsal tomorrow. And I'll make a deal with you...

If they're not fine, I'll take over. But I don't want to, because I watched you today and you were stunning."

She turned to give me a hug but she was crying harder than ever. "I can't believe you're being nice when I've been so horrible to you."

"We've both been horrible – and stupid!" I said.

She laughed through her tears and started to move away. "I'd better go."

"See you at dinner then, Cara."

"Yeah…and thanks for making me feel better."

Mia was in the mood to celebrate when I got up to the dorm, because the exam was over and she thought she'd done well enough to at least pass.

"Just think, no more practicing or horrible exams for ages!" she said, dancing around.

Grace held her hands and they did a cute little dance together. "And no more gym competitions or volleyball matches!"

Jess and I were laughing like crazy. "You're supposed to love all your sports and music, you two! What's going on?"

Mia flopped onto the bed. "Yes, I do love it really."

"It's just nice when the pressure's off," agreed Grace.

"How did your scales go?" I asked Mia.

"Good, I think. So you see all that testing you did paid off!"

When we'd talked about the rest of her exam she asked how the rehearsal had gone and I told her what had just happened with Cara. The others all tuned in and everyone gasped when I said Cara had been crying and I'd had to reassure her about her performance.

"It must have taken real guts for her to come and talk to you like that," said Naomi thoughtfully when I'd finished the story.

"Yeah, and she must have been hurting like crazy inside," added Mia. "When you told her you thought she was stunning this afternoon, did you really believe that?"

"Um...well she was almost as good as she's always been."

Naomi put her arm around me. "I'm really proud of you for giving her back her confidence when she's been so horrible to you."

Then Mia opened her eyes wide. "*And* you could have done both performances, but you're sticking to sharing the role! That's why *I'm* proud of you!"

"Yes, good old Georgie!" said Katy. "That was really...grown-up."

"Well, thank you," I said jokingly, "but actually I can only manage short bursts of acting grown-up, and right now I need to be my usual immature self, so who's up for a game of Twister?"

Mia laughed and chucked the Twister mat on the floor. "Good! I'd hate it if you turned sensible the whole time because I'd miss the crazy old Georgie too much!"

After dinner there was just one more sensible thing I had to do that day. I caught up with Camilla and Savannah coming out of the cafeteria but didn't talk about Cara until we were outside.

"She's really lost her confidence," I said, "because she thinks you prefer *my* interpretation. But it was *her* performance that inspired me to be able to do the role, so I think we ought to support her, don't you?"

"But you're better than she is!" said Savannah. "I can't act half so well myself when Cara's playing Amy, and that's bringing the standard of the play down."

"Savvy's right. You should be doing both nights,

you know," said Camilla shaking her head and looking worried.

I didn't tell her that that was what Cara thought too. "Look, it was her first time acting for ages and she must have been really anxious about how she was doing, and then when everyone seemed so flat and Miss Pritchard said what she said, if I'd been Cara at that moment I would have felt absolutely awful. It was no wonder that she kept stumbling."

Camilla looked down and Savannah heaved a big sigh but neither of them said anything so I went on in a quiet voice, not really knowing if I was doing any good.

"If you could only...kind of...reassure...her... then her acting would automatically get back to how it was before."

After a few seconds Camilla looked up, and then suddenly broke into a giggle. "I don't know about you, Savvy, but I feel as though we're being told off by a sixth grader!"

Savannah smiled. "Don't worry, Georgie, we get the message. We'll try to make her feel more confident at the technical, okay?"

I felt like dancing back to Hazeldean, calling out, "Mission accomplished!" at the top of my voice. But that would have been too crazy even for me, so

I just strolled back at my usual lazy pace feeling happy that at last everything was as it should be. Well, okay I was late for study hour and I didn't have a clue how to do it, but hey, what's new?

Chapter Ten

It was seven twenty-two on Saturday night. Eight minutes until the curtain was due to go up. I was standing in the wings feeling the most nervous I'd ever felt in my life. I knew Mom and Grandma and Roxanne were somewhere out there. They knew I had a main part but they were going to get the shock of their lives when they saw just how big the part was. But it would be a nice shock, hopefully.

I tried to clear my mind of all thoughts of everything except the actual play, because that's what Miss Pritchard had told us to do. Savannah, Camilla, Rebecca and a couple of others were all waiting in the wings too, but none of us were talking because we were focusing hard on getting into role, letting ourselves slide into our characters so we truly felt as though we *were* those people. I was finding it pretty hard because my mind wouldn't stop going over the events of the last two days.

The technical rehearsal had taken place during school time so I hadn't been able to watch it, but Cara and I had agreed to meet in the courtyard afterward, and she'd come rushing up, given me another of her big hugs and said she felt much happier because it looked like Savannah and Camilla had gotten used to having her back in the role of Amy after all, as they'd acted wonderfully and said "Great job!" to her at the end.

The dress rehearsal had been great because the play totally came to life with everyone in their costumes. The excitement leading up to the first Friday evening performance had been crazy and I'd sat in the audience with all my friends and felt nervous for the actors, especially Cara. But I didn't have to worry. It was a big success with tons of clapping at the end, followed by Ms. Carmichael making a speech to thank everyone for coming, and thanking Miss Pritchard and all the actors for their hard work. So, of course, the applause grew even louder after that and Cara actually winked at me from the stage.

And now it was about to happen all over again and I was the one who was brand new to it all, standing behind the curtain with my makeup on, and listening to the audience's excited chatter.

"Break a leg, everyone!" said Miss Pritchard, appearing in the wings before she had to rush off to watch us from the front row. Then she blew a kiss into the air, which made us all smile the tiniest of nervous smiles, and a minute later the curtain went up and the show began.

I don't think any two hours in my life have ever gone as fast as those two hours, which is so totally unfair because I wanted them to go on forever and ever, it was so utterly exhilarating, to use a word that Savannah taught me. In the interval we all talked at the tops of our voices in the green room behind the stage, while Savannah had a makeup change because she had to look deathly pale for the second part. Then the few of us who were on at the beginning of the second half went back to the wings and got into role again.

When it came to the part where I'm so sad about Beth dying, I really forgot where I was until I heard someone in the audience do a little sob, and I realized the tears were rolling down my face. Savannah was crying too and for a moment neither of us could speak so we just hugged each other tight and then someone else in the audience sounded as though they were crying. It was awful. But wonderful. And incredible.

And then it was over and we had to take our bows. We four sisters were the last people of all to bow, and when we ran on the stage the clapping seemed to turn to thunder and people started to stand up, until in the end the whole audience was on its feet. Lots of the girls were whooping and cheering, including my friends, who were all sitting together with some of their parents. I scanned the rows for Mom's face, but it was hard to see because of the lights glaring in my eyes, but then I spotted Roxanne standing on a seat and saw that Mom was on one side of her and Grandma on the other, and...wow! There was Dad too, clapping up high and grinning at me with such a proud look on his face.

Even when Miss Pritchard appeared on the stage and stood between me and Savannah with her arms around our shoulders, the clapping didn't stop, so in the end she had to raise her hands for silence. Then the house lights went on so we could see the audience clearly, and she made a really moving speech telling everyone how wonderful their daughters were and praising all the staff who'd helped with the production, and finishing up with the story of Cara being sick and how I'd stood in for her, and then Cara had gotten better so we'd finished up sharing the role. As she spoke I thought how straightforward it all sounded, but only three people in the world knew how complicated and emotional it had all been. Cara wasn't even there, but Mia was, and she gave me her best smile, then started off a new round of applause.

There was complete bedlam after the speeches were finished because all the actresses rushed into the audience to be with their parents. Roxanne ran toward me for a hug, with Mom not far behind, then Grandma kissed me and finally Dad gave me a big bear hug. He said that Miss Carol had made a special phone call to Mom to tell her she'd heard that my dad wasn't going to be at the play but she thought he might want to change his mind because she understood from the drama teacher that I was a real sensation. And Mom had explained to Miss Carol that the moment Dad had heard I'd gotten a big part he moved mountains to get back a day early from his business trip.

"But the drama teacher was right!" he added,

shaking his head as though he couldn't believe it. "You were a total sensation!"

I laughed. "I'm glad you thought I was good, Dad, because then when I show you my grades, you might remember that at least I'm good at something."

My laughter petered out when I saw the serious look on Dad's face. Oh dear, perhaps that wasn't the right moment to bring up my grades.

"Georgie, we were chatting with your friend Mia before the show started, and she explained a little about what you did to cheer up that girl, Cara. So, by my reckoning that's two A pluses you've got! One for drama and one for life skills, which is the most important subject of all, I might add!"

Dad had tears in his eyes when he said that and as I leaned against him, Mom wrapped her arms around both of us and spoke into my hair. "I'm so proud of you, Georgie!"

Then suddenly Mia was right there at my side. "Oh Georgie you were fantastic!" she said, jumping up and down. And I thought for the thousandth time how lucky I was having a best friend like her, especially one who could get me A pluses from my dad.

* * *

Later Mia and I went up to the dorm together. I was about to go inside when she stopped me.

"What?" I asked.

"Anything different around here?" She was flicking very unsubtle glances at the sign on the door.

I looked at it, expecting to see the alteration I'd made, but instead I saw another alteration. This is what I read.

Katy the Queen of Style
Grace the Sportswoman
Jess the Artist
Mia the Musician
Naomi the Wise One
Georgie the Best Actress in the World

And for some reason the sight of those words made me want to cry. "I didn't think you'd noticed I'd changed it," I said in a wavery voice.

"Course I noticed!" said Mia looking indignant. "We all did! But *you* obviously didn't notice that *I* changed it again, because it's been like this for the last week! You were fantastic with Cara and you were fantastic in the play!"

"You're pretty fantastic yourself, Mamma Mia," I said, from the bottom of my heart.

And at that moment my whole world shone brightly as though I was standing in the beam of the most glittering golden spotlight. My very favorite place to be.

Turn the page for some School Friends fun from Georgie!

School Friends Fun!

I t's great going to school at Silver Spires, because I get to be with my friends all the time! Why not organize a special night for all your friends to get together too? I've got some fabulous ideas for fun stuff you can try, and they're all to do with my favorite thing...acting!

 ## How to hold a movie night

Even if you don't like acting yourself, I bet you like watching other people do it, so a movie theme night is great fun for everyone! Apart from watching your favorite movies, there are great games you can play that will definitely give you all the giggles. Just pick a theme, grab some DVDs...and don't forget the popcorn!

★ The theme for your movie night could be anything – comedies, musicals, or maybe your favorite actress or actor. Once you've picked one, you can stock up with DVDs, decorations, and even get your friends to dress up, all according to your theme. So ballgowns all around for Hollywood night!

★ Play the Who Am I? game! Put the name of an actor or actress on a Post-It note and stick it on your friend's forehead so they can't see it. Then they have to ask yes or no questions (like "Have I ever won an Oscar? Was I in a movie with Keira Knightley?") to figure out who they are. How many questions will it take them?

★ Entertain your friends with your best impression! Do a famous line, or even act out a whole scene from a movie and see who's first to guess the title. Whoever gets it right gets the next turn!

★ Have a competition to see how many movies each person can think of that feature a particular actor or actress – whoever gets the most wins. (And I always think chocolate's a great prize!) You can try other themes too, for example, how many movies can you think of with a color in the title?

So what are you waiting for? Grab your friends and have some School Friends fun!

Georgie x

Now turn the page

for a sneak preview of the next

unmissable *School Friends* story...

Rivalry
at
Silver
Spires

Chapter One

I love this moment of walking through to the school pool from the changing room. My whole body comes alive, even more than it does on the athletics field. Maybe it's something about the smell, or the steamy atmosphere, or the beautiful pale green water that reminds me of the sea back home in Thailand. Whatever it is, I love it. I always find my footsteps speeding up, because I'm so desperate to get into the water and swim and swim. But this time Jess's hand on my arm stopped me in my tracks.

"Grace, look!" she said in her dreamy voice. Her eyes were on the far window, which goes all the way from the floor to the ceiling. "Look at that sun shining in. Isn't it beautiful? The water looks like liquid gold up at the deep end, doesn't it?"

I smiled at my best friend. "I bet you'll do a painting of that later, won't you?"

But she didn't answer because she was lost in a little Jess-daydream. By now there were quite a few people in the pool. I hadn't seen anyone diving in yet, though, so I decided not to do that either. It might have seemed like I was showing off and that was the last thing I wanted anyone to think.

Mrs. Mellor, our wonderful PE teacher, was hurrying people out of the changing room while the lifeguard sat on high and watched over us all. I went down the steps and felt the cold water rising up around me, and although it made me shiver, it was a shiver I loved. It took me straight back to swimming in the sea in Thailand over the Christmas break. This is the beginning of spring at Silver Spires, which is the most perfect boarding school in the world, and here I am about to start our very first swimming lesson, because we didn't have any actual scheduled swimming before Christmas. I should be totally happy, but there's just a small chunk of happiness missing because I can't help feeling a little homesick. My mom and dad and my big sister seem so far away when I'm at school. I know I've got my amazing group of friends, including my very best friend, Jess, and I also know I'll soon be back in boarding-school mode, but it's only the first year of boarding for all us sixth graders so we're still getting used to it.

"Oh no! This is torture!" came good old Georgie's voice. I glanced over to see her hunched up at the top of the steps.

"The quicker you get in, the quicker the torture – as you call it – will be over!" said Mrs. Mellor firmly. She clapped her hands. "Chop-chop, everyone! Five minutes' free swimming to get used to the water and then we'll start the lesson." She went over to help someone tighten their goggles, then turned back around. "Georgie Henderson, your challenge is never to be the last one in the pool."

Georgie didn't answer, just hunched her shoulders even more and folded her arms, while her best friend Mia jigged up and down in the pool in front of her. "You'll get used to it really quickly, honestly!" I heard her say, as I set off to the deep end, doing front crawl.

I was concentrating hard on making my body as narrow and straight as possible, bringing my arms right over my head and cutting through the water with the side of my hand, while keeping my legs and feet strong. My parents wanted me to have swimming coaching during the break but in the end I only had three sessions because our wonderful Christmas celebrations went on for so long this year, with lots of visitors and outings. It was hard leaving those hot sunny days of fun behind and coming back to the winter chill at school.

When I got to the deep end I stopped and looked around. If I half closed my eyes the surface of the pool looked like pale green silk with lots of brightly colored balls floating all over it. We have to wear caps for swimming and each boarding house here at Silver Spires has its own color. My five close friends and I are in one of the sixth grade dormitories in Hazeldean House and we've all got purple hats. The girls from Willowhaven wear green hats, Beech House wear blue, Forest Ash, red, Elmhurst, white and Oakley, yellow. I love it that girls from all the different houses are mixed together completely randomly for things like sports and music and art. Then for math, science and English classes we're in first, second and third sets.

Mrs. Mellor blew her whistle to announce that we only had another two minutes of free swimming and I suddenly realized I was starting to shiver because I'd been still for a while and wasn't fully warmed up. I set off back to the shallow end doing the fastest crawl I could manage and then turned around and headed straight back to the deep end, trying to do the proper breathing on every third stroke, but not managing it very well because breathing for the crawl stroke is my biggest weakness. I'd almost completed the second length when, through the blur of the water, I noticed a blue hat coming up on my left. Someone from Beech House was swimming really fast. We touched the side at exactly the same time and when she turned to face me, I realized it was a girl named Felissia Streeter. I smiled at her, but all I got back was a cold stare and I felt horrible shivers pushing through the nice warmth I'd gathered during my hard swim. I didn't know what that look was about and I don't like it when I don't understand things.

Mrs. Mellor's whistle made me jump and I was glad that I had to concentrate on listening to instructions about lining up at the deep end because it took my mind off Felissia's horrible look. The rest of the lesson was great fun because Mrs. Mellor always makes everyone feel so confident, and we tried all the different strokes, even butterfly, which I'm hopeless at. I loved all the other strokes and didn't want the swimming lesson to end.

"That was great fun," said Jess, in the changing room afterward.

"I wasn't very good," said Georgie.

"Neither was I," added Naomi. "I just didn't seem to ever get warmed up."

"I thought you were really good," said Katy, who's Naomi's best friend. She grinned at me as she rubbed her hair with a towel. "But we knew you'd easily be the best of our group, Grace."

Jess shuffled closer to me on the bench. "We're so lucky having you in our house," she said.

"And we've got Katy too," I quickly pointed out, because Katy's a strong swimmer.

"Are you two joining the swim team?" Mia asked.

We weren't sure whether just anyone could join the team, because the team isn't a fun thing like a club. It's much more serious. So Katy went to ask Mrs. Mellor. She came back with the answer that if you want to do the swimming competition you *have* to join the team, but anyone's allowed to sign up for it and see how they do. "But *you've* definitely got to join, Grace!" she added. "You're the best!"

"With some luck you can enter *all* the races, Grace, and the rest of us can just cheer you on. Then

Hazeldean will be the winning house! Yay!" Georgie was pulling her sweatshirt over her head so we could only just make out what she was saying, but the others all laughed, apart from Jess. She probably guessed I'd be feeling anxious about all this praise because I'd already told her I didn't feel as confident about swimming as I did about other sports.

"There are some really good swimmers in the other houses," I said quietly, and I couldn't help glancing around for Felissia. I spotted her in front of the mirror scooping her hair up into a ponytail.

"Felissia Streeter's good, isn't she?" said Mia, who must have followed my eyes.

I nodded and suddenly felt tempted to tell the others about Felissia's look, but I didn't because it would have sounded like such a silly little thing. And as soon as I'd had that thought, I realized that actually, that's exactly what it was – a silly little thing – and I told myself to stop being silly and forget about it.

But just before bedtime it popped back into my head again. We were up in our dormitory admiring each other's bulletin boards. Jess's was covered with photos she'd taken during the holidays, but they weren't the usual kind of photos of people or scenes; they were all of different sorts of trees, like close-ups of gnarled old bark, or thin bare trees silhouetted against the white sky. She's got such a big imagination, Jess has, and I really love the way she looks at the world. We're so different from each other and we both think that's the very thing that makes us best friends.

Katy's board was artistic too, but in a different way. Hers was covered with fashion pictures, because that's Katy's biggest passion. Naomi's had photos of elephant and deer roaming across stretches of scrubland with barely anything growing. That's because she comes from Ghana in Africa. In fact, it's easy to forget that Naomi is actually a real live African princess. She's so modest and never boasts about it at all. Her family lives here now but she still thinks of herself as Ghanaian and I knew she'd been back to Ghana over the holidays because she mentioned a charity that she's working for called Just Water, which helps the people of Ghana to have access to clean water. Naomi and I had also talked together about how far from home we both felt, and how cold winters are here compared to our own countries. We're not the only ones who come from far away though. There are girls from all five continents at Silver Spires.

Georgie was admiring the way Mia had made

photos of her pets and her family into a collage.

"When I tried to do that with my pics, I chopped off half the heads!" she said, frowning. "And what's the point of having the best actors in the world right over your bed if they're headless?"

"Do you want me to rearrange them for you?" asked Mia.

But Georgie was standing in front of my bed by then, hands on hips, pretending to be disapproving. "Don't say we've got to look at a bunch of athletes again, Grace! Is that all you think about – sports?"

"You're only jealous, like the rest of us, Georgie!" said Jess.

Georgie's eyes shifted from my board to me. "Yes, I *am* jealous! Why can't I look like Grace? I'd love to be slim and fit. I wish I could run like a deer and jump like a...like a...kangaroo."

I laughed. "I hope I don't look like a kangaroo when I'm jumping!"

Georgie ignored me. "And I'm very jealous of your fantastic swimming too!"

Naomi put her arm around me. "Yes, we've definitely got the best swimmer in sixth grade in our house!"

Katie rubbed her hands and grinned like a

mischievous little girl. "I bet the other houses are green with envy!"

"Don't say that," I quickly told them, feeling myself getting anxious again. "I'm not all that good at swimming, you know. There are lots in sixth grade who are better than me. I'll have to train like crazy."

"Nonsense!" said Katy. "You're just as talented at swimming as you are at every other sport!"

All this praise was exactly what I'd been dreading. That's why I'd felt tense every time I'd thought about the swimming competition during Christmas. It was due to take place before Spring break, and with all the training I wanted to do, that didn't seem far enough away. It's a horrible pressure when people expect you to do well at something, and it's not only my friends, but my parents and the teachers here too. You see, I came to Silver Spires on a sports scholarship, which means that my fees for the school have been paid because the school thinks I'm going to do really well at sports, so that when we have inter-school competitions I'll win and that will make other schools admire Silver Spires. I don't feel so much pressure when it comes to other sports like volleyball, because I'm confident about them. But swimming's different. I'm not so good at swimming.

I had to make the others realize. "No, honestly, I'm not just saying it. At home my sports coach says that swimming is my weakest thing, so I've made a resolution to train hard. Only, it might not make much difference, you know."

"You can only do your best, can't you?" said Naomi, who's the wise one of the group. "And remember you'll have swim team as well."

I looked around hopefully. "I'm not going to be the only one doing swim team, am I?"

"Well, don't look at me!" Naomi laughed. "I'm allergic to cold water."

"Me too," said Mia, wrinkling her nose.

"The trouble is, it clashes with fashion club," said Katy, "because it's on Wednesdays. Oh, by the way, Mrs. Mellor said they're not meeting for swim team this coming Wednesday though, because she's away."

Then Jess surprised me. "I might come," she said, her eyes looking dreamy as they so often did. "I enjoyed floating on my back and staring at the ceiling in the lesson today. It's got an incredible pattern on it, you know, like an optical illusion."

I had to smile. "You're such an artist, Jess! Imagine noticing the swimming pool ceiling!"

"Okay, that's enough swimming talk for one day!"

Georgie suddenly announced. "I'm off to the computer room."

Everyone decided to check their e-mails then, so we all trooped down two flights of stairs to the computer room.

"Good, we're the only ones here!" said Katy. "One computer each."

"We've only got a few minutes before we have to get ready for bed," said Mia, who gets even more anxious than me about rules and regulations. I don't know about Mia, but for me I think it's because my parents brought me up pretty strictly and always expect me to respect my elders.

"Yay! Loads of people online!" said Georgie, who's really into the Silver Spires chat room at the moment.

The rest of us were quickly checking our e-mails. I had a long one from my mom, and although it was nice to hear from her it made me feel a little homesick too. Out of the corner of my eye I could see that Mia had finished on her computer and was leaning on Georgie, watching her screen.

I'd almost finished reading Mom's e-mail when I suddenly heard a gasp from Mia.

"What?" I heard Katy ask.

There was no reply and I glanced around to see that Mia's eyes were wide and worried.

"What are you looking at?" Naomi wanted to know, and a few seconds later we were all bunched around trying to read the message on Georgie's screen.

Someone with the username *Torpedo Gal* had written, *Shame about the big show-off who just has to be best at everything she ever does, including swimming.*

"That's not very nice. Who's written that?" asked Mia.

Georgie didn't answer at first, just started typing back. *What big show-off?*

We all watched the screen as the message came back. *You should know. You'd better warn her that we don't like show-offs and it's about time she gave someone else a chance to win.*

"So who *is Torpedo Gal*?" asked Naomi.

"I don't have a clue," said Georgie, in a surprisingly quiet voice. "I've got so many people on my contact list I don't know who I'm talking to half the time." Her voice faltered. "But whoever it is knows who *I* am."

A horrible prickly feeling was creeping up my spine.

"But who's she talking *about*?" asked Katy.

There was a small silence, and then everyone must have clicked that it could only be me. Georgie turned around and gave me a kind of apologetic smile, at the same time as Jess's arm went around my shoulder, and the prickly feeling spread right up to the backs of my eyes.

To find out what happens next, read

Rivalry
at
Silver
Spires

About the Author
Ann Bryant's School Days

Who was your favorite teacher?

I had two. Mr. Perks – or Perksy as we called him – because when I was only eleven, he let me work on a play I was writing during class! When I was older, my favorite teacher was Mrs. Rowe, simply because I loved her subject (French) and she was so young and pretty and slim and chic and it was great seeing what new clothes she'd be wearing.

What were your best and worst classes?

My brain doesn't process history, geography or science and I hated cooking, so those were my least favorite subjects. But I was good at English, music, French and PE, so I loved those. I also enjoyed art, although I wasn't very good at it!

What was your school uniform like?

We had to wear a white shirt with a navy blue tie and sweater, and a navy skirt, but there was actually a wide variety of styles allowed – I was a very small person and liked pencil-thin skirts. We all rolled them over and over at the waist!

Did you take part in after-school activities?

Well I loved just hanging out with my friends, but most of all I loved ballet and went to extra classes after school.

Did you have any pets while you were at school?

My parents weren't animal lovers so we were only allowed a goldfish! But since I had my two daughters, we've had loads – two cats, two guinea pigs, two rabbits, two hamsters and two goldfish.

What was your most embarrassing moment?

When I was eleven I had to play piano for assembly. It was April Fool's Day and the piano wouldn't work (it turned out that someone had put a book in the back). I couldn't bring myself to stand up and investigate because that would draw attention to me, so I sat there with my hands on the keys wishing to die, until a teacher came and rescued me!

To find out more about Ann Bryant visit her website: www.annbryant.co.uk

Secrets, hopes and dreams...

School Friends
are forever!

Welcome to Silver Spires

Katy is nervous about going to boarding school for the first time, especially as she's got a big secret to hide. The girls in her dorm seem really nice, but when someone sets Katy up, how will her new friends react?

Drama at Silver Spires

Georgie loves acting and is determined to win her favorite role in the school play. But her audition goes wrong and an older girl steals the show instead. Will Georgie ever get her chance in the spotlight now?

Rivalry at Silver Spires

Grace is at Silver Spires on a sports scholarship and feels the pressure to do well in competitions. But when someone starts writing hurtful messages saying she's a show-off, she loses her nerve. Can she still come out on top?

Princess at Silver Spires

Naomi hates the attention that comes with people knowing she's a princess. But when she's asked to model in a fashion show, she can't refuse – after all, it's for her favorite charity. What could go wrong?

Secrets at Silver Spires

Jess is really struggling with her classes. She can't ask her friends for help, because she doesn't want them to find out she isn't as smart as them. But now that she's being made to go to special classes, how long can she keep her secret to herself?

Star of Silver Spires

Mia's ambition is to be a real musician. She'd love to enter a song she's written in the Silver Spires Star contest, but then she'd have to play live onstage too. And performing in public is her biggest fear ever – can she find the courage to overcome it?